She turned around . . .

She heard something like a creak. Like one of the crates opening. Then another, louder—followed by a thud. Rachel's heart started beating faster. Other sounds then. A scratching noise. The sound of something moving—of nails hitting the wood floor. A dog sound, she thought.

She knew she wanted to run toward the door out. But she had not moved. And now, with that doglike sound, there was something else. A dull, slapping sound, something fleshy slapping against the floor.

She took a step. The sarcophagus watched. Another step. Then she heard the growl behind her. It wasn't a dog growl. She turned. She began shaking.

She saw the paws of the animal, and the long black claws. But it wasn't a dog. No, it had a long, pointed snout, open, teeth bared and glistening. Then Rachel noticed the rest of the animal.

She saw how the furry body suddenly changed midway to pinkish skin, how the back of the animal ended in dwarf-like legs, ending in human feet.

I have to run, she thought. Have to get the hell out of here.

But the creature, as if reading her mind, opened its jaws. As if saying . . . try it.

Try to run.

On three, Rachel told herself.

One, two—

And then—

All the lights went out . . .

POLTERGEIST
THE LEGACY

Maelstrom

MATTHEW COSTELLO
BASED ON THE TERRIFYING HIT
TELEVISION SERIES CREATED BY
RICHARD BARTON LEWIS

ACE BOOKS, NEW YORK

POLTERGEIST: THE LEGACY™: MAELSTROM

This is a work of fiction. Names, characters, places, and incidents are either the product of the author's imagination or are used fictitiously, and any resemblance to actual persons, living or dead, business establishments, events or locales is entirely coincidental.

An Ace Book / published by arrangement with
Tekno•Books

PRINTING HISTORY
Ace edition / February 2000

The Penguin Putnam Inc. World Wide Web site address is
http://www.penguinputnam.com

Check out the ACE Science Fiction & Fantasy newsletter
and much more on the Internet at Club PPI!

ISBN: 0-441-00711-2

ACE®
Ace Books are published
by The Berkley Publishing Group,
a division of Penguin Putnam Inc.,
375 Hudson Street, New York, New York 10014.
ACE and the "A" design are trademarks
belonging to Penguin Putnam Inc.

PRINTED IN THE UNITED STATES OF AMERICA

10 9 8 7 6 5 4 3 2 1

POLTERGEIST
THE LEGACY

Maelstrom

PROLOGUE

The Bermuda Rise, November 1947

I t's a toy, Andrej thought.

The freighter *Maroc* had suddenly turned into a toy, sloshing around in a great gray tub of churning water, a toy ready to be flipped over.

He huddled below decks listening to the sickening groan as the ship dipped forward then reared up again as if it might fly—and all the while the metal of the ship groaned under the pressure, the terrible stress of an angry sea playing with it.

This toy ship . . .

He held the gun close, its muzzle next to his cheek. Not that he would ever turn it on himself. He wouldn't do that. No matter what happened. It was a great sin, a mortal sin that would condemn him to hell for all eternity. And hell must surely be worse than this.

Now the ship heaved starboard as if whatever giant was playing with it had decided to give it a real ugly shake. A shake to see what falls out. Then Andrej felt a rock to the port and—yes!—the ship began another dip into a wave trough.

Andrej was glad he couldn't see it. He had sailed all his long life and never, ever experienced a sea like this. This was beyond any storm he had ever faced. It was demonic. He crossed himself, beseeching whatever power God still had in this region to help him. He prayed to stop the mad waves, the terrible wind, the screaming of the metal.

But more than that, he prayed for the strength to start moving.

Because if he didn't start moving soon, it would be over.

Andrej knew where he was. They had been nearing the Bermuda Rise under the secrecy of night. Their captain had sailed the freighter out of Cairo on a dark, moonless night secretly bound for the North American coast. The captain didn't trust Andrej with their destination. He just instructed him to steer the ancient oil burner for America.

Now, the captain was dead.

So were most of the others.

Most? All? Andrej didn't know. And now he shivered, thinking, *What if it is only me? What if I am the only one left and—*

Another dip into the sea, and this time Andrej could sense the bow sinking deep into the gray embrace of the wave, diving into it like a drunken sailor going for a deadly swim. And Andrej could almost feel the sea outside, muffling the noise, surrounding the stressed metal, eager to keep it, hold it, crush it.

Come on, Andrej thought. *Let her go. Please, dear good, sweet God, let the bow come up.*

Because if it didn't rear up the other side of the wave, if the bow remained buried in the wave . . . and another wave broke, engulfing the rear of the small freighter, then the ship would be sucked down into this terror . . . this horror of sea and wind.

Andrej waited. He licked his lips. The metal of the ship called out to him with its song of pain. He waited. The cool barrel of the gun rested beside his cheek.

No, he thought. *It's not coming out.* In a second the ship would flip over and water would rush in, eager to claim all

2

the dry areas before pulling it down to the sandy bottom of the Bermuda Rise.

But then, like one of the proud stallions he used to watch on the hills in Yugoslavia, the ship lurched up, rearing up, free, fighting. But Andrej knew that the ship couldn't fight alone. There was no one at the wheel. The ship bopped this way and that, while the wheel spun crazily out of control.

The captain was dead. More than dead.

Which meant that Andrej had to make his way topside to what passed for a bridge on the freighter. Get to the bridge, try to out-think the waves, move the ship off the Rise, out to deeper, steadier seas. If there was any steadier sea.

And one other thing.

Don't get killed.

Don't let what happened to the captain, to the others happen to me, Andrej thought. *Use the gun, and the flashlight, and—God . . . somehow—get to the wheel.*

Amazingly, Andrej stood up. Below decks stank of oil and salt and thousands of cargoes. Andrej held the gun out in front of him. He took a step. Another. *I have to get to the wheel,* he told himself.

Every step felt like a major victory.

Closer. But then, when the toy ship was once again shaken, he'd lose ground, stumble, and—sometimes—even fall onto the oily floor.

He somehow reached the narrow staircase that led to the small crew area. Above was a tiny kitchen, the crew's quarters, the captain's room. And bodies. *Is that all,* he thought? Is that all he'd find? If everyone were dead, if they all killed themselves, then he'd be okay. No need for a gun, nothing to be afraid of . . .

Step by step, up the stairs. He moved deliberately, steeling himself for the butcher shop above. He could smell it even before he reached it, the bodies in the narrow hallways, some desperately sprawled at the doorway to their staterooms.

He moved down that hallway, telling himself that he wouldn't look in any of the staterooms. This journey would be much too hard to do if he looked. But once past the first room, he looked in the second and saw a scene that made his long-empty stomach heave. One of the crew lay on the floor, a young Algerian boy. His body looked . . . exploded, as if someone had fired a cannon from within his belly.

Andrej's stomach clenched. The smell was awful. Then, the bow of the ship did another crazy dive into an incoming wave, and Andrej stumbled forward, slipping not on oil but the syrupy blood of his shipmates. He fell to his knees, which became sodden with blood.

Now the ship reared, threatening to send Andrej flying back to the staircase, tumbling down to the hold.

Must move, Andrej told himself. *Must get up, keep moving. There's no danger. They are all dead. Yes, they killed each other, all of them. I'm alone, on this horror sea. And I'll be dead if I don't get to the wheel.*

Somehow, he got to his feet and stumbled to yet another set of stairs. This time he didn't look into the end cabins, knowing that only worse scenes waited inside.

Then up, his feet slippery from the blood. It was hard to climb the rocking stairs and hold on to the gun. But he had to hold on to the gun. He couldn't let go.

As the bridge came into view, he tried to remember how it had happened . . . and what had happened.

Later, he told himself. Later he could try to figure out what had happened. Later there would be time to think.

He was topside, standing in a protected entryway facing a door that led to the small bridge and beside another door leading to the hell outside. The wind shrieked constantly here, a steady scream as if some demented creature was howling, enjoying the ride. And coming fully out to the passageway, Andrej got to see the next wave . . .

It was a wall of water.

The height of the wave was only visible due to the white caps that lined its top, a frothy icing that let Andrej gauge the mammoth height of the wave. He spent another few precious seconds watching. *It's fifty feet,* he thought. *At least. Maybe more.* Taking its own time, roiling toward the small freighter. Big enough, Andrej knew, to take the ship

4

down, especially if the wave behind it was close enough to come and gulp the stern.

Andrej stuck the revolver into his pants, using the belt as a holster.

Then he grabbed the railing to his left with two hands. The white of his knuckles glistened in the dank light. But all the time he kept his eyes on the great wave charging toward the ship.

And this time he got to watch the ship do its terrible dive. First the freighter tried to climb the slope of water. But then the wave broke over the bow, and suddenly the ship was under water. Completely.

He heard a scream—long, loud, horrible.

It was his own voice, screaming through the entire wave. His hands locked on the railing were the only thing that kept him from flying backwards. Then the ship began to right itself, still rocking left and right.

But that attack was over—only for Andrej to see another wave, like a demented warrior coming toward him. He looked ahead to the wheelhouse, and saw the wheel spinning.

He spun back to look at the wave, bigger than the last one. Was that his imagination or was it truly larger? If it was bigger, when the ship began its climb, it could make the ship go vertical—and then—and then . . .

The stern would slip into the trough made by the water, the *Maroc* would flip over, perhaps get crushed into pieces by the wave, or, or—

He stumbled to the wheelhouse. There were only seconds. But each second seemed such an immense, tremendous amount of time. Yes, there was plenty of time to wobble his rocky way to the wheel, grab it, and then try to figure out if there was any way the small freighter could cut into the wave and survive.

He looked ahead.

The wave wasn't as close as he thought.

No, it was further away; it just looked close since it was so . . . huge, moving toward the ship, a gray mountain magically animated, filled with a deadly malevolence. The wall of water had been far away, and now that it was closer, he could see that it was still growing. Not merely fifty feet tall. Not merely sixty feet tall, but seventy feet, maybe even taller.

He felt like weeping. Holding the wheel, attempting to steer the ship was . . . pathetic. He reached down to the throttle. The engines were already on full. Still, like a good sailor, he held the wheel as he felt the first sickening tug tip the ship upwards, beginning its dreadful climb. Now all he could see ahead was the wall. But this time the shape and slope of the wave made it so that the ship's bow didn't cut into the wave.

This time, the ship rode the wave up.

How big? Andrej wondered. God, how tall was this mountain of gray, churning water. Because if it was too big . . .

The ship tilted back . . . a 30-degree angle, then growing, 40, 45 degrees like some demented water roller coaster. The wheel in his hands felt as though it controlled . . . something. But that was an illusion.

Higher, God, to a sickening 50 degrees and the gray in front of the bridge's window had given way to a frightening blackness—the black-gray night sky, as the *Maroc* pointed its nose nearly straight up.

The moment of truth arrived.

Would the ship ride the crest of the mammoth wave, or—

The answer came too quickly. The black sky above seemed to freeze, then a terrible groaning noise echoed from the stern and Andrej felt the ship slipping backwards. The giant wave was so large the *Maroc* was nearly vertical and now the stern was in the mouth of the trough, slipping into it, sinking backward.

Andrej grabbed the wheel hard.

He knew what would happen next.

The ship flipped. Like yet another ride from one of the traveling carnivals that visited his town of Brest, the ship slipped back, turning upside down. For a moment, Andrej dangled from the wheel, the deck of the ship now the ceiling. Until the ship crashed into the sea upside down, the wave pummeling the bottom. From the sound, Andrej imagined the hull cracking in a dozen places.

The battle was over.

Now the ship was a helpless cork on the raging sea. *But,* thought Andrej, *I'm alive. I'm alive. I can still survive this.*

As if in response, the sea shot into the small wheelhouse. Giant tubes of water rocketed at him from three directions, pushing his body left, right, down all at the same time.

Until the room was completely submerged.

There was no light.

No air. But Andrej found himself remarkably lucid. It was as if something wanted him to live. *I've survived . . . everything, even this!* There had to be a reason. All he had to do now was swim out to the door. Grab a life preserver, swim outside, and try not to think about the raging mountains of water.

Andrej turned around. He couldn't see anything, but he knew that the wheel was behind him . . . so the door to the top deck was only feet away.

The other passage, leading to the stairs below decks, was to his left. And for a moment, Andrej thought of the floating bodies below, the blood mixing with the sea. A beacon to any hungry creature that prowled the Bermuda Rise.

He kicked once, twice. His hand locked on the latch to open the door. How many seconds had he burnt, how many seconds more could he hold his breath before the burn in his lungs became intolerable?

It was impossible to tell.

He pressed down on the unseen latch. Nothing happened. Again, and—

He could see something.

A glow, from behind him that slowly turned the blackness into the murky outline of the door, the latch handle, and—

He looked over his shoulder.

The glow came from below. Yellow-orange. Flickering, seemingly warm, strangely inviting, seeming almost warm.

His hand locked on the latch. He pressed down.

Until the other door to the bridge opened. And Andrej saw things moving in the water, looking like strange sea creatures from a nightmare. They were body parts . . . each suffused with the same yellow-orange glow. A forearm and a hand wriggling through the water, clutching to propel itself. A leg kicking, then—God—the captain's mangled torso, moving, impossibly horrific.

Like a butcher shop come to life.

Andrej's hand was locked on the latch.

Then a sickly swimming hand grabbed him, as if to make him pull open that latch and free these . . . things to the sea.

And Andrej would have done that. He would have opened that door, and tried to get away with the consuming urge to stay alive. His lungs burned now, only seconds away from the drowning reflex, that moment when the body demands resolutely that a breath must be taken—even if it's a liquid breath of burning salt water.

He would have pulled down on that latch.

But then there was this sound from above, from the hull—or what was left of it—the thundering bellow of the sea hammering down.

And this time the wheelhouse and the entire ship was smashed downward under the weight of the crashing water, the violent mountain-sized waves cross-cutting each other.

The floating pieces in front of Andrej became a blur as the *Maroc* shot down thirty, forty feet. Rocketing down, so far down, away from the surface, away from the air.

A golden-orange hand clutched at Andrej's shoulder.

At that hand's end, bloody red tendrils trailed away, lit by the glow.

I'm in hell, Andrej thought.

The fire in his lungs roared. Until there was only one thought, even as those fingers crawled up to his throat.

Breathe. There was one last second of resistance—even as he felt the ship plummeting down. One last second and then he opened his mouth.

And there, in the deep temperate waters of the Bermuda sea, Andrej sucked in the water as if it was life-giving

8

oxygen. For a moment his lungs were pleased, gorged on the salt water. But then he coughed out the water only to gasp more water in.

It took minutes, this process of breathing the unbreathable.

Minutes, watching the horrors dance around the room, trapped, falling. The golden-orange glow faded.

Until—

It's over, Andrej thought.

His mind turned foggy.

Over.

And for him, it was.

PART ONE

Gathering Clouds

ONE

D erek turned to Alex who was hunched over her computer, lost to her research. *This is what she loves to do best,* Derek thought. Alex was great in the field, but she was absolutely brilliant in this room.

"Alex?" Her head didn't budge. "Alex . . . maybe it's time for a walk? Some fresh air?"

The she looked over. "Sorry, Derek. I was just checking on some reports out of Oman. Remember those amphorae that were found? Already the department of antiquities has put a security blanket on the whole thing."

Derek got up and walked over to Alex's terminal. "If I know you, that won't stop your digging."

Alex laughed. Derek valued her more than she knew, certainly more than he could say. Such things just didn't come easy to him. It was one thing to wrestle with issues of faith and superstition, to look into the abyss. It was quite another to be at ease with the people you cared deeply about.

Maybe, he thought, *it's because I know I could lose any*

of them, all of them. Maybe there's no room for any real emotional connection.

"How's Nick getting on?"

"Oh, he sent an e-mail this morning before diving."

Derek raised an eyebrow. "Vacation? Didn't know I had authorized it."

"Oh come on, Derek. He needed some R&R. After that dreadful business in Baja. He shouldn't have gone there alone."

"Yes . . . I should have listened to you."

Baja. A simple fact-finding mission, A cult led by this modern *brujo*, a rhasta. Except that the *brujo* actually had some powers—he could tap into some ancient force tied to the Mayans. His followers nearly killed Nick. Worse, the *brujo* disappeared into the Yucatan. That was one thing Alex was now scanning for, using their network of contacts, official and otherwise . . . to see if there was any news of this leader.

"You're right. A few days relaxation would be good for him."

Alex nodded. "He feels terrible. And we can ill afford to lose him. Not with Philip out of the loop."

Derek shook his head.

"Philip will be there when we need him."

Alex turned back to her screen.

"When will we *not* need him?"

She grabbed her mouse and continued searching the Net.

The sun glinted on the choppy Pacific, catching the feathery white plumes. Nick looked back at Luis steering his small dive boat. Luis had taken Nick out for his very first dives nearly twenty years ago. And here he was, still working the chilly waters off Catalina. "I don't need warm water to dive," he always joked. "Just give me the big fish, face-to-face. That's what real diving is about, eh?"

How old was he? Nick remembered coming back after his SEAL training to visit Luis. The man, old even then, had been enjoying a Dos Equis, sitting on his ramshackle porch overlooking the Pacific. Nick told him about all the advanced technology, nitrox, re-breathers, using mixed gasses for depth . . .

Luis always nodded indulgently, like a parent listening to some fantastic tales from school. "How deep," Luis asked, "do you really have to go? I have been nose to nose with a gray whale at sixty feet. I've taken you down . . . one hundred thirty . . . one hundred forty. That is plenty deep." Another sip of his beer, refusing to acknowledge that the world has changed. Then again, with finality, "Plenty deep."

This dive was a quick run to the spot Luis called "The Canyon," for—hopefully—a quiet, peaceful time underwater. Baja had been a mess. Nick knew he screwed that up—but he could have used better information from Derek. Now the *brujo*—the charismatic spiritual leader—was gone, lost to the jungle, to reappear somewhere else.

Screwed that one up, Nick knew.

The ship bounced awkwardly, catching a choppy wave at a bad angle. The old boat landed hard and the air tanks rattled in their sleeves.

But there was another reason Nick wanted to do this trip. Luis was old. He had just about let his dive business fade away. Luis preferred watching the other, faster boats take the diving *touristas* out while he sat in the shade of his porch watching the ocean water change colors.

Wouldn't be long, Nick knew, before Luis—and that part of his life—was gone forever. Like his father.

This time, though, Nick wanted to make sure he said everything he had to. There was so much time for regret, very little time to actually say those things you want to.

Another hard slap rocked Nick as ship met sea.

He looked back at Luis, who grinned. With his leathery brown skin, he seemed almost part of the rough, splintery wood of his ship. "The sea is angry today, eh, Nick? Someone must have pissed in her!" Luis laughed, then repeated, "Must have pissed in her!"

And Nick laughed. It was good he did this. There would be plenty of time to go back to Frisco and face Derek. plenty of time to deal with the Legacy.

But not much time for this.

• • •

Father Philip kissed the chasuble and slipped it around his neck. The altar boy, James—one of the stars of St. Pat's basketball team, a gangly six-foot-one and growing—stood at the entrance to the altar, waiting for the early Mass to begin.

Whenever Philip doubted his decision to leave the Legacy all he had to do was look at kids like James, or the faces of his parishioners, mostly poor inner-city people whose faith was a real treasure. The Church stood for hope and, Philip believed, support and understanding in a world that grew harder every day.

Philip straightened the chasuble and he noticed that there were some loose golden threads near the bottom. They seemed symbolic of this church, a little tattered, in need of replacement or repair. But the Church is more than the building or the vestments. The Church was its people . . . the people and their spiritual leader.

Being here, I know why I'm alive.

Philip picked up the chalice and walked to the passage that led to the altar. He nodded to James, who followed closely behind.

He walked out to the altar and faced his parishioners. There weren't a lot of people on this Tuesday morning. A scattering of faces, most of them old, a few young mothers. *It can't be easy for any of them to come here,* Philip thought. *To worship together, to ask God's help, His love.*

Inside this holy building, the dark forces that the Legacy fought seemed far away, puny almost. *The house of God is a mighty house,* Philip thought.

He put the chalice down while James stood to his side. Philip raised his hands in the ancient, traditional gesture of a blessing.

"The Lord be with you," he said.

And the parishioners murmured the words of response, a blessing on their priest, on Philip. "And also with you."

The ancient ceremony of community and mysticism, the Mass, began.

• • •

Luis idled the ship and scuttled back to the anchor. He picked the anchor up, his arms still powerful enough to easily hoist the heavy chunk of metal.

The ship rocked back and forth.

"The sooner you're in the water, the better, Nicky."

Nick pulled the back zipper of his wet suit tight.

"You're not diving, Luis?"

"No. Not with this water so . . . choppy. The ship might pull free of the anchor, drift off to Hawaii. I best stay on board."

Nick nodded. Of course, what Luis suggested violated one of the cardinal rules of diving—never dive alone. But Luis also knew that Nick was a trained Navy SEAL diver. There was no emergency that Nick would face that he couldn't deal with alone.

Still, he wished Luis would dive with him.

One last time . . .

As if he could read Nick's mind, Luis said, "Go, Nicky. Then we head back and have some nice beers together."

Nick nodded. It would feel great to enter the near-weightless condition underwater and forget about everything in the cold waters of the Japanese current. "You're just getting too old, eh, Luis?"

Luis laughed. "I'll out-dive you any day, Nicky. And out-fuck you, too!"

The man laughed full out, the sound booming even in the open expanse of the water. Nick smiled. This was good.

I need this, he thought.

He slipped on his fins and then slipped his arms into his buoyancy-control vest. He pulled the Velcro sash tight across his chest and then yanked down on the shoulder straps, tightening them. He shot some quick bursts of air into the vest. He gave the regulator a test suck. Tasted as foul as ever. All the equipment was Luis's, all of it years out of date. No state of the art here. But all serviceable, well maintained by the old divemaster.

The boat gave another violent lurch.

"Ready, Nick?"

17

Nick got up, hoisting the tank strapped to his BC out of its sleeve.

"Yup." Nick rocked on the weaving boat. "Could you get the sea to calm down? I'd like to jump in the water, not get thrown in."

Another laugh and Luis looked up at the deep blue sky. "I'm afraid that's not up to me."

Nick waddled to the back of the boat, sat down on the back. He slipped on his face mask and put his regulator in his mouth. Another test, and then he took it out.

"See you in thirty!"

Luis gave Nick an "okay" sign, and Nick rolled backwards, into the churning sea.

Philip lowered the host and broke the pieces into the chalice. He looked at the tiny flakes of bread, now pronounced to be the body of Christ. He looked up. Everyone sitting out in the church believed that. An amazing miracle—a small sliver of bread is transformed into something all-powerful and mysterious.

Philip didn't question the miracle.

There weren't many things he questioned anymore.

The parishioners started lining up at the altar railing to receive communion. Philip took the chalice filled with hosts and, with James trailing behind, he went to the railing, sharing the sacrament with the parishioners.

To each person who knelt before the altar, their tongue outstretched or their hands open, Philip looked into their eyes and whispered "Body of Christ."

He moved down the line of people, but there was nothing rote or mechanical about this. He felt blessed to be able to be here, to feel the intensity of these people's faith.

"Body of Christ." He said, then moved to the next person, fulfilling the ancient ritual.

Until—

He came to a person whose mouth wasn't open.

Whose hands weren't outstretched.

A young woman, her eyes shut tight. He hadn't noticed

her before. Her jet-black hair and fair complexion spoke of another neighborhood, another country.

Philip waited. There was something wrong with this.

"Miss," he said.

Philip waited.

Then, he felt a cold breeze. But the morning was warm, almost hot. Philip shivered. He looked at the line of parishioners. They seemed frozen, a tableau. Philip's hand tightened on the chalice, his other hand held a host. The woman opened her eyes.

But where there should have been eyes, there were only black sockets. Philip stepped back. He held the sacred host tightly. The woman looked at him . . . looked at him though she had no eyes.

And she spoke. A hoarse whisper that seemed to travel on the chilly current of air that filled the church.

"I am not lost," she said.

Philip turned to James but he, too, seemed frozen into position, standing by the railing, perpetually ready to resume his duties.

"Father," the eyeless woman said, "Father. Please. Remember this. I am not lost." The woman's voice was gentle, soothing. Reassuring. What was happening? What had transformed this place of sanctity and refuge into this nightmare?

The woman closed her eyes, and when she opened them, the black pits now glowed, fiery, tiny flickers of flame snaking out.

"Father . . . Father . . . are you all right?"

Philip turned to the altar boy who looked scared.

"What, I—"

Philip turned back to the woman. But now she was—of course—gone. In her place, an old black woman held her rosary, fingering the tired, worn beads. The woman, lost to her prayers to the Virgin Mary, didn't seem to take notice of the priest.

"Father, are you all right?"

Philip nodded. The church was once again warm, and the sunlight sent shafts cutting through the upper stained-glass windows, catching a million dust motes in the morning.

"Yes. Just felt a bit . . . dizzy, James." He nodded at the young basketball star. "I'm okay now."

Philip extended a host to the old woman kneeling before him. "Body of Christ."

And the old woman stuck out her tongue . . . while Philip, still shivering, wondered what he had seen, what it might mean.

Twenty feet down, Nick checked his gauges. His air was fine and his dive watch looked okay. The water was cold, hovering just above 60 degrees, cold even for these waters off Catalina.

Nick wore a full three-quarter-inch wet suit and hood, so he was warm enough. But he wished Luis were here to enjoy the dive with him.

He kicked around and headed nose down, equalizing his ear pressure easily. It felt wonderful to be weightless and free, soaring down into the shallow canyon below. *Maybe I'll get lucky,* Nick thought. *Catch sight of a gray whale, maybe a hammerhead or two, a big turtle.*

He checked his gauge again. Fifty feet down, and the water temp slipped below 60 degrees. *Brrr . . . the Caribbean, it isn't,* Nick thought. Down another ten feet, and he saw the v-shaped cleft of the canyon. Luis had discovered this place nearly forty years ago, a narrow, shallow trench favored by smaller fish, which in turn attracted the bigger animals.

As if on cue, Nick spotted a loggerhead turtle kicking swiftly just above the trench. Nick got on the turtle's tail and the turtle kicked into higher speed. The turtle hurried on, but Nick was faster, his big fins giving him an unfair advantage until he could easily reach out and touch one of the black flippers of the turtle.

There, thought Nick. *Got you. Tag, you're it.*

Enough hassling the turtle.

And Nick stopped giving chase. He checked his gauge again. One hundred feet. The trench started here, and then snaked west, heading to the deep ocean, quickly dropping to 120, 130, 140 feet with every fin kick.

If you got distracted, you could find yourself slipping into deeper water, to a place where the nitrogen would quickly build up in your bloodstream and make you giddy with depth. Rapture of the deep was dangerous even for an experienced diver who knew the signs.

Nick looked at the wall of the trench, a coral outcrop currently grazed for tiny organisms by some silvery fish that took no notice of Nick. A small mottled crab scuttled away.

The sandy bottom of the trench looked as untouched as the surface of the moon.

A shadow crossed Nick.

At this depth, a good amount of light and color starting at the red end of the spectrum vanished, soaked up by the water. But there was enough light filtering down to tell you if something came between you and the sun.

Nick looked up. It wasn't one thing that blocked the light, but a trio of hammerheads. These sharks usually minded their own business. They looked fierce, with their anvil-shaped head and rows of teeth below, but they were about as benevolent a shark as existed.

Nick stopped and watched them circle above him, as if playing in the columns of the sun's rays filtering down the water. They seemed more like porpoises, so relaxed in their lazy circling of the water.

Then—Nick felt something else.

As if he was being watched.

It was a diver's intuition. When you dive with large animals, in their world, you gain a sense of when you're not where you should be, when something's looking at you, perhaps considering an attack.

He turned around.

And there was another shark. Only this was a tiger shark. A shark known to attack people. The tiger was more of an attacking animal than the Great White.

It was thirty feet away, maybe closer, as it weaved left

and right. Nick reached down for his dive knife strapped to his left calf.

He slipped it out of its sheath.

How big was the shark? Looking at it head-on, Nick couldn't tell. But the shark's snout was aimed right at him, the teeth a dull yellow in the pale bluish light at 120 feet.

Nick looked down. Perhaps he was just in the tiger's way. He turned upside down and kicked even deeper into the narrow trench. In seconds he was between the two walls of the canyon. He looked back up. The shark was gone. Just a commuter traveling the underwater fast lane.

Then the shark hit.

The snout rammed into Nick's back and razor-sharp teeth scraped at the neoprene, easily ripping shreds of the black material in strips off his back. Nick felt the oddly distant sting of his skin being cut and then the sting of salt water touching his open wounds.

He spun around with the knife and, without even taking aim, he swung the blade out in front of him. The water around him quickly grew murky with his own blood. But then his knife hit something, followed by a violent yank as the shark reared back, pulling away.

And when the shark pulled away, it yanked his knife with it.

Shit, thought Nick. He looked at his gauge. Air was okay . . . good for another five minutes or so. But he was at 140 feet. Just at the edge of where things can get dicey, especially if you were breathing normal air and not nitrox.

Nick had no knife. He figured that the shark was probably between him and the surface.

He waved at the water to clear away the murky cloud, but it only seemed to make the visibility worse.

If the shark had hit his arm . . . or even a leg, it might have been all over. The shark could have locked its powerful jaws around the limb, clamped down, and then played with Nick like a toy, shaking him this way and that until exhaustion and blood loss killed him.

The tiger couldn't get his jaw around his torso.

That saved Nick's life. For now.

He floated in the reddish cloud. He couldn't stay here much longer.

Nick had to move. But not until he knew what the hell he'd do if the tiger returned.

And Nick knew this . . .

When there's blood in the water . . . a shark always returns.

TWO

Derek flipped open his cell phone. "Hello."

"Hello, Derek." It was Philip.

"Philip, good to hear from you. How goes things at—"

"Derek, something happened this morning."

Alex walked out of the Data Center and looked at Derek. Derek held up a hand indicating that Alex should stay.

"What happened?"

Derek listened as Philip explained his vision, his hallucination, whatever it was. "Philip—I don't want you to take this the wrong way . . ." Derek looked over at Alex. He had such a knack for saying things . . . wrong. "But have you been working too hard? I know you, throwing yourself into every aspect of parish life, counseling, working with the homeless, fighting the Oakland city council—"

"Derek . . . listen to me. I'd like nothing better than to be free of everything the Legacy stands for. But this vision was like a warning—someone, something reaching out to me."

"Can I put you on speaker? Alex is here."

"Yes." Derek pushed a button and replaced the receiver.

"I mean, the woman kneeling at the railing in front of me was as real as anyone else coming for communion. When I looked at her eyes, I felt as though I could have staggered right into them."

"Philip, Alex here—did anyone else seem to see anything?"

"No, that's just it. There was this moment where time stopped. And only I saw the woman. The altar boy was at my side. He saw nothing."

Derek circled the room. He felt bad for Philip. He so much wanted to be doing God's work, to serve others. He was totally driven to serve. Yet things conspired to bring him back to the Legacy. But what was this . . . vision? A warning? A threat?

"And you remember," Derek said, "only those few words—'I am not lost'? Nothing else?"

"Nothing. Only her words, 'I am not lost.' It was so plaintive. As though if she didn't let me know that she wasn't lost, she might vanish, into the blackness of her eyes."

"But what of the fire?" Alex said. "You saw flames in her sockets? Did they seem . . . threatening?"

A pause. Philip was obviously reliving the moment. Derek felt the chill.

"No. I felt no danger. Not from her. But I felt this terrible sense that she needed help, that she was trapped between the blackness of space and—I don't know—the fires of hell."

Philip's words hung in the room for a moment. There was something about his words, his imagery, that seemed right. And Derek felt worried for the young priest who so much wanted to get away from all this.

But then a high-pitched chime echoed from the speakers of Alex's computer terminal.

"Philip, I—"

Derek watched Alex turn back to her machine.

"What is that sound?" Philip said.

Derek walked behind Alex who had already hit a key, then another.

25

"Oh," Alex said. "I don't like this." She turned to Derek. "Derek—what is it?" Philip asked again.

It would take a minute while Derek absorbed what he saw, and told Philip the incredible thing that had just been picked up by the Legacy Data Network.

Floating in the murky water, Nick knew he had to move.

He was down too deep and the throbbing he felt in his head signaled the nitrogen build-up in his blood.

And where was the tiger shark? Would he try to surface only to swim right into the shark?

Nick thought then of one of his Navy trainers, Jake, a good old boy from Mississippi who helped create the SEALs' Advanced Underwater Program. Jake told the group a story about diving off Tortola, doing some practice rebreather dives, deep dives, while working on underwater explosive tests.

They were at two hundred feet, maybe a bit more. Crystal clear water, but they were down so deep that the color had leeched out leaving only blues and purples.

He turned to look for his buddy. And Jake saw that he was alone.

But not really, as he saw something wriggling its way toward him. Something dark and big, with only tiny flashes of white up front. A Great White. Rare for these warm waters. Then Jake saw, to the side, a smoky cloud. Only, as Jake told it, he knew that it wasn't any cloud.

Blood at this depth isn't red. His partner had been taken silently, pulled away, ripped apart, eaten—and now the shark was coming for him.

There was almost no time to react. But Jake told his class how he tugged on the safety line three times, signaling that something was wrong, that he was coming up.

Three tugs, and then the Great White's snout was right there.

And Jake told Nick and the rest of the trainees that he did the one thing you could do, the only thing.

He raised his arm to protect his head. The shark took the arm like bait, and then began using the captured forearm to shake Jake around. Funny, he told them, he felt almost nothing, just the strangely distant sensation where his arm was locked in the shark's mouth. There was this weird passivity, as if everything was so hopeless that there was no point in doing anything.

Then—a few more shakes, dizzying rattles—and a crunch.

Jake told the young SEAL divers that he looked down— and half his arm was gone. The shark pulled back, and for a moment nothing more happened.

But then he hit his BC, inflating the vest, rocketing to the surface, streaming blood behind.

At any minute he thought the Great White would swoop from beneath him and snatch him by his fins.

And, Nick thought, Jake knew that everyone in the small classroom had their eyes on the empty right sleeve.

Jake said something then, something that—unfortunately—stuck with Nick now as he prepared to bolt to the surface.

"Gentlemen . . . there's nothing in the world like knowing that you are being eaten." He paused, letting the concept sink in. *"Nothing."*

Nothing, Nick thought. And he took a deep breath and began fin kicking to the surface.

"Derek, you still there?"

Derek stood behind Alex looking at the screen of the Legacy Data network. The LDN was their private worldwide network designed to flag strange and unusual events anywhere in the world. The network fed off the hundreds of news servers around the world. The LDN also relied on the worldwide network of friends and allies—a priest in Belize City, a Greek scholar in Venice, hundreds around the world—all of whom served as the Legacy's early warning system.

This item, though, was picked up by the Network's own search engine.

"Philip—do you have e-mail at the rectory yet?"

Philip laughed. "Yes. We only just got indoor plumbing,

but I don't go anywhere without my laptop. What did you get?"

"We just got this from the Network, Philip. A young woman in New York vanished three days ago and her parents did this interview . . . saying that she seemed scared of something at work, something supernatural."

"Could just be hysterical parents."

Derek said, "Still, the picture of the girl looks exactly as you described—I mean, based on what you said . . ."

"I'm e-mailing the photo now," Alex said.

"Let me hang up. I do only have one phone line."

"Right. Speak to you in a moment."

The line went to dial tone. Derek walked over to the conference phone and hit the disconnect button.

"There we go," Alex said.

Derek walked back to the monitor and looked at the picture. Even in black and white the young woman was stunning, with lustrous black hair and dark eyes. Derek looked at her name, "Martina Popov."

As Derek looked, he thought of the words spoken by the specter that appeared to Nick . . . "I am not lost . . ."

And standing with Alex, they waited for Philip to call back.

The first few fin kicks didn't seem to take Nick anywhere.

There was no way to judge how far he had traveled—or if he had moved at all. He couldn't see the swirl of his air bubbles and he couldn't see if the deep purple-gray water was turning lighter.

He considered just bolting . . . popping air into his BC, dropping his weights, and rocketing to the surface as fast as he could.

But then he'd get bent. No question about it, a fast emergency ascent from this depth would cripple him with decompression illness, might very well kill him. And there was no guarantee that the tiger shark wouldn't enjoy plucking at a fast-moving target.

So he kicked nice and steady, as the water cleared.

Until he could look up and see—maybe forty, fifty feet

above—the shimmering mirror of the surface.

Going to be okay, he thought. *I'm going to make it.*

Which is when Nick looked below and saw the tiger corkscrewing his way to him, his knife still buried in the side of its body. And Nick thought of Jake's story. *Nothing like that feeling of being eaten, turned into some other creature's . . . food.*

Nothing at all.

He kicked harder—but it was no contest. The tiger was capable of terrific speed. It would have him in a second.

He kicked again.

Catching something with the tip of his fin. *How much will I feel this, he thought?*

Any second now, the teeth, the tremendous jaw power.

Then—shadows from above.

Quickly, Nick looked up.

To see: three dark clouds swirling above him.

The hammerheads.

Want some of me too? Nick thought.

Let's make a bad dive . . . really bad. One for the record books.

But the hammerheads, swimming with an almost balletic precision, circled Nick, swimming a smooth ring around him. He watched the massive hammerheads, their black eyes separated by a fleshy anvil, circle him.

What was going on?

Nick looked down. Some water seeped into his mask, blurring the lenses. But as he looked down he saw the trio of hammerheads circle below him, down to the tiger shark, and then—in unison—the three sharks attacked the tiger.

Hammerheads weren't fierce fighters like the Great White or tigers. But they rammed into the tiger one after the other, first from this direction, then another. Nick kept rising, all the time looking down on the amazing spectacle below.

The tiger slowed to defend itself, snapping at one hammerhead and tearing into one part of its head. But then a second hammerhead bit into the tiger's dorsal fin and pulled it back. Soon, blood filled the water as the lone tiger and the hammerheads wrestled below, biting, tearing . . .

Nick kept rising while the carnage below faded. Like a dream.

Like some great diving story, a tale exaggerated to impress a girl.

He looked up.

The smooth mirror of the surface was only fifteen feet away.

I should stop, he thought. *Do a safety stop. Give my blood some time to vent the nitrogen.*

That's what he knew he should do. But he kept on going. There was no telling who might win the battle between the tiger and the hammerheads.

He broke the surface and popped more air into his vest. The sky was still a crystalline blue. He turned around, searching for Luis. The small dive boat was a good surface swim away. Nick waved his arms at Luis.

Come on, Luis, he thought. *I don't know how long I have before the shark comes after me.*

Nick saw Luis turn and wave back. Luis asked Nick a question by making a big O with his arms.

Okay?

Nick, bobbing in the water, made a big O back. He heard the start of the motor and Luis quickly brought the boat over to Nick. He reached down, smiling and grabbed Nick's fins then helped him aboard.

As soon as Luis saw Nick's back—the deep lacerations made by the tiger's teeth—he ran for the boat's first aid kit. *"Madre de Dios!* What happened?"

Nick sat on the small seat, nesting his nearly empty tank into a vacant sleeve.

He looked at the choppy water. It was usually so calm here.

"Nick, tell me. What went wrong down there?"

Finally, Nick turned and looked at Luis. "I'm not too sure."

The choppy water gave no sign of the strange battle perhaps still being waged below.

"I'm not sure at all . . ."

THREE

Jerome Farrand tapped his pipe against a small oak tree. He looked at the rolling hummocks of the farmlands of Kent, milky white in the near-full moon that had just crested a small hill to the east.

He thought, as he often did, of the ancient history of this countryside, the simple peasants who farmed the land then futilely tried to defend it from the Roman invaders who put England on the map. *Such an ancient, blood-stained land,* Farrand thought, hitting the base of his pipe one more time against the tree. But not that ancient—Farrand had breathed air that was twice as old as any Roman ruin you could find in all of Great Britain. He had touched the leathery preserved skin of Egyptian mummies that were already a thousand years old before the first Anglo village ever existed.

That was—of course—from his own distant past.

Farrand didn't try to think much about his previous life. He was an old man—seventy-eight—and as each year passed, simply getting up in the morning seemed to grow harder.

He dug out his tobacco pouch, the tan leather rubbed to

a baby-soft smoothness. He looked in the pouch, the moonlight bright enough for him to see that he had enough for maybe one more small smoke. A few quick puffs. *Just as well,* Farrand thought. *Smoke too much, anyway. And drink too much. An ex-cleric's complaint. Get a priest hooked on that first jolt of wine at Mass, and you have an oenophile for life.*

Farrand missed saying Mass. There was something incredibly reassuring about going through the same ritual every day, something done by rote and loaded with reassurance. But it was Farrand's loss of his belief in just that reassurance that made the Mass, the Church, God—all of it impossible.

Farrand knew way too much to stay a priest.

He struck a match, the flame starkly bright in the milky light.

Even to stay a Jesuit, he thought, grinning to himself.

Once he met a priest who had been . . . there. Been at that world-famous exorcism in Georgetown. Later that event, the myth, would be turned into a novel by a writer who went to the school, and then turned into a noisy film filled with vile language and blood and vomiting.

The real event, the priest told Farrand, had been far worse.

It had been, the priest said, a probe.

Not an isolated event, but an attempt to open a gateway. Had that little girl been allowed to remain possessed, then the forces of evil would have gained an important beachhead.

Farrand never forgot the priest's face when he talked about the event. He saw things that no one should ever witness. No night's sleep would ever be the same.

Farrand had been relatively young then. His own life's work, his own discoveries in the scorched Valley of the Kings, lay ahead.

And now, behind him.

He puffed on his pipe, the smoke a thing of delicate beauty as it curled away from the pipe and arched up to the treetops.

It was over for him, he told himself.

Then, with the bit of the pipe clenched tightly in his mouth, he gazed at the brilliant moon and whispered the same prayer he did every night . . .

Please . . . God . . . let it be over for me.

Derek opened the door to the Luna Foundation.

To the casual outsider, the impressive building looked as though it was merely another well-financed think tank. And though funding wasn't something Derek worried about—there were always those who would contribute to hold back the darkness—there were still times he had to make a late night call to a rich benefactor or two.

When he needed the funds, he'd call the people who knew that the work of the Legacy must not be disturbed.

"Philip, so good to see you!"

The young priest, once an active member of the Legacy, entered the doorway with the hesitation, Derek thought, of a wayward son returning home. Philip's reasons for wanting to leave had been many and complex. To come back now, perhaps in need, perhaps scared, couldn't be easy.

"Derek, thank you for setting this up."

Derek put a hand on Philip's shoulder.

"You will always be welcome here, Philip. You didn't expect that your work for the Legacy would be forgotten?"

"Sounds like I've been working for the Mafia," Philip said, smiling.

Derek laughed. "Exactly!"

He clasped an arm around Philip and led him into the mansion, up the stairs, to the nerve center of the Legacy.

"Is Nick coming?"

"I left a message on his pager. He may still be diving. He had a bad time with some business in Baja. He's taking a few days off. I can bring him up to speed later."

"And Rachel?"

Rachel Corrigan, the newest member of the Legacy, came to them when the Fifth Chest was uncovered in Ireland. A practicing psychiatrist, Rachel initially rejected everything the Legacy stood for. But when demons threatened her own daughter, her duty became clear. If not easy.

"She's in New York. A psychiatric conference. We can probably get her on the phone."

Philip shook his head. "Probably no need. At least not yet."

Derek nodded. "Good, come—let me show you what Alex has found."

Philip nodded and looked at Derek. "I'm just glad that I'm not crazy."

"Me, too."

They reached the holographic portal, the "wall" that sealed off the inner chambers of the Legacy. They walked through the hologram, and on into the Communications Center.

Farrand stood in the center of his small room situated above what used to be a barn. After decades traveling the world, this rural life suited him. If nothing else, he was spared arguing with his Jesuit superiors, trying to warn them of what may happen.

And then . . . when he started to talk to his superiors about his fears, about the patterns he saw wherever he went—whether at the Mayan ruins of Tikal or the Great Pyramid of Cheops—they turned a deaf ear to him. And that was funny. Here they were, entrusted with defending humanity from the forces of darkness, and they closed their minds to such a real threat.

After decades, the Jesuits were glad to see him go.

Farrand even heard stories that some priests questioned his sanity. A young priest, a religiously trained psychiatric counselor, was ultimately assigned his "case."

My case, Farrand thought, looking at the moonlight spilling into his room. He imagined the jokes that made the rounds in the religious conferences.

Did you hear about Farrand? Too many excavations! He went around the bend.

He tried to argue—to explain—what he believed could happen . . . what *would* happen. But it was too late. This was the modern Church. He was lucky that they even believed in God.

And what did Farrand believe about God? Did he believe in an all-knowing being that loved and cared for humanity? Or did he believe in some entity that couldn't be bothered with whatever evil transpired on earth? At this point, Farrand wasn't sure what he thought of God.

Or vice versa, he thought.

He knelt down in the moonlight.

He felt cold.

Then, kneeling on the hardwood floor, he wondered: why all these thoughts tonight? And he hoped he didn't have those dreams, those terrible nightmares that made him shoot awake in the middle of the night, sweating, sometimes even crying.

Why tonight? he thought.

He prayed silently, but his lips moved, the words, the pattern soothing. He prayed until the moonlight crept past the window and the room was once again dark.

Derek turned to Alex, indicating that she had the floor.

"The woman's name, Philip—the woman you may have seen—is Martina Popov. She was born in Russia, near Vladivostok, and was brought to this country in nineteen eighty-one when she was fourteen. Her parents settled in Brighton Beach."

Derek looked at the large monitor on the table showing the picture of the family.

"Her family joined the burgeoning Russian community there." Alex hit the mouse button, and another image popped up, a graduation picture of young Martina, darkly beautiful.

"That's her. Younger. She's even more beautiful now," Philip said.

"Yes. She could have gone into modeling. Instead, she went to Columbia on a full scholarship, majoring in ancient history. She got her MA, also from Columbia, in archaeology, specializing in ancient civilizations."

Another mouse click, and a picture of an art gallery

35

called Okthoro. Just visible in the window, a display, "The Secrets of Ancient Sumer."

"She became a special assistant to this gallery's director, Dr. Anna Whitney."

"Must be a smart girl," Philip said quietly.

"Brilliant, I imagine," Derek said.

Another click from Alex. And there was a story from the *New York Post*.

Young Historian Missing, the headline read.

"Then, three days ago, she left the SoHo gallery for her parents' home. But she never arrived. Dr. Whitney said Martina had left early, saying she had some errands. Her parents never saw her again."

Philip muttered something.

"What, Philip?"

" 'I am not lost.' That's what she said. I am not . . . lost."

Derek looked at Alex. Their eyes made contact. Philip was obviously shaken by his vision. He waited for the young priest to ask the obvious question.

"Why me?" Philip said.

There was a sound from behind, someone coming into the room.

They turned to see Nick, walking stiffly, his face grim, set.

"Nick, I thought you were taking some days off and—"

"I heard what Philip just said . . . 'why me.' " Nick made a small laugh. "I can top that. Let me tell you what happened to me, and then maybe you can answer that question for both of us."

Nick walked over to a chair and sat down, grimacing.

"What happened?" Derek said.

"Just about the most amazing thing I've ever seen, Derek. And I might be crazy, but maybe it has something to do with what happened to Philip. And if it does, we better find out why real soon."

Farrand was asleep. At least, he thought he was asleep.

He floated in that dream state, that not-quite-sure state of being awake and lost to another land.

In his dream, he saw the couple downstairs, the good people who ran the farm and rented him this small room. The woman and man both with burnished, wrinkled faces carved by years of outdoor work in the brusque English air.

He saw them talking.

So real—

And then the woman looks outside the window, pulling aside the lace curtain, and then says something to her husband.

Farrand can't hear what she says. It's a dream. A silent dream.

But the husband wanders over and looks out the window, and then his face changes. A look of confusion, of concern. They both turn and look at the door.

The front door.

So real . . . it was as if Farrand was there.

He had a thought. *Don't go to the door. Don't open the door.*

That . . . wouldn't be good.

But the husband, Frank, his cheeks ruddy from the warmth of the room, goes to the door and opens it.

And there's a man there.

Smiling at them, talking. Frank and his wife exchange glances, looking at each other . . .

The man at the door smiles. Then he reaches toward the husband as if to shake his hand. But the man's hand transforms as it stretches toward the husband, turning into a bony-white hook, the claw of a bird of prey. It happens so slowly in the dream.

Frank doesn't shake the claw. Instead the claw hand jabs forward and then rears up, hooking the farmer like a fish, spearing him. His wife recoils, she screams, a silent dream scream, her mouth wide open—

Farrand shot awake, bathed in sweat.

Hearing the scream.

Downstairs, the woman howled like a terrified animal. Other sounds echoed up to the dark room, liquid noises.

Farrand slid off the bed and pulled on his pants. He saw his wallet on the bureau. He stuffed it into his back pocket.

He pulled on his shoes. All happening so fast, this moment rehearsed in countless nightmares.

Except this is no nightmare.

He knew who the man was. And none of this was a dream. Another terrible howl, and Farrand knew that the woman was being jabbed now, her small life horribly snuffed out on the wooden floorboards of her living room.

Farrand stood up. He looked at the door that led to the back stairs. He remembered Frank telling him—complaining—about how they required a fire ladder of some kind if they let the room out.

The door led to a ladder.

Farrand took a step, still feeling so sluggishly half-asleep. One step, then another, wondering how much time he had before the man—the creature—downstairs caught up with him.

He opened the door. He heard a footfall behind him.

The man whose hand had turned into a claw was coming for him. The people downstairs were innocent. Farrand thought he was foolish to think that here, he might be safe.

There is no "safe," he thought.

The small door opened to the night air. It was brilliant outside, lit by the moonlight. Farrand hurried down the stairs, his old, brittle bones protesting at the speed. One misstep, a fall, and it would be too late. And despite his recent arguments with God, he prayed.

Let me escape, Farrand thought. *Let me escape. Because if it's beginning, they will need my help.*

So many things to think about, he thought. But all of them would be pointless unless he got away.

Down the stairs. Nearly to the bottom.

Behind him, he heard the door to his room being kicked in.

Farrand ran.

He was old. But every morning, when the sun was just above the hills to the east, he hit the foot trails and cow lanes and jogged. It wasn't much of a jog, not more than a really fast walk. But he kept at it, every day. Sucking the damp, morning air through his nose. Hating the stupid exercise, but knowing that he'd have to be as healthy as an old man could be.

So he trotted now, but not onto one of the trails. That would be obvious.

He ran into the thick of the small stand of young oaks that girded the farm. As he ran, he replayed the warning of the dream—the image of Frank being ripped in two by the clawlike hand—and the sound of the screams.

"Thank you," he whispered. "Thank you for the vision." *I won't,* he promised as he puffed his way through the dense woods, *waste this chance.*

He kept praying as he ran, looking over his shoulder once, then again—until a root caught his foot. He fell face forward, hard onto the packed ground. He spun around as if something was ready to pounce on him.

But it was quiet.

Get up, he thought, *Start running. Think,* he thought, *Think of what must be done.*

The moon disappeared behind a giant cumulus cloud. The woods turned even darker. And Farrand was grateful.

Derek and the others listened to Nick's story, their faces reflecting their relief that he was okay—but also a deeper concern . . . what did this mean?

"I . . . felt as if these other sharks, the hammerheads, were watching over me, protecting me. I mean, it's weird, they were—"

Philip finished the thought. "Like angels?"

Nick nodded.

Derek got up. He had a concern he wasn't sure he should share with the other members of the Legacy. Two members had been somehow touched by unusual events. The first question that had to be answered was whether these events were related. And if they were, what was happening? Where did these visions come from? What did they mean?

Derek wondered if his fellow members of the Legacy were being—somehow—contacted. But what for?

It was not a situation that Derek liked. He needed to

know more. He had no choice but to commit his forces to learn more.

"Derek, what are you thinking?"

He looked at Alex. Alex occasionally got flashes of insight, bits and pieces of precognition from somewhere. But now she was strangely quiet. That was worrisome. Alex's sporadic ability could be helpful. But so far she had been silent. And Derek wasn't inclined to press her.

"So," Derek said, "we need a plan."

Philip spoke up. "We have to learn more about this young woman, Martina Popov. Maybe talk to her parents, and the gallery director."

"Yes. But who—"

"Rachel!" Alex said.

"What?"

"Rachel is already in New York at an American Psychiatric Association convention. Bored to tears, she told me last night. Brighton Beach isn't far. She could also go to the gallery."

"Great. We can keep doing research on the network here."

"I'll help with that," Philip said.

"Signing up again, father?" Nick said. Philip rolled his eyes.

"I said 'help.' I didn't say that I was rejoining the Legacy."

"Make sure you bring your holy water."

Derek looked at Alex. The tension between Nick and Philip hadn't dissipated in the time Philip had been gone. Derek guessed that it was too much to expect that it would. Nick and Philip lived in two different worlds.

"I'll call Rachel. Nick, why don't you get some rest. You still look weak."

Nick looked as if he was about to argue, but then he nodded.

Derek looked around at his team. He thought, *I don't know what's happening here. And that frightens me.*

And for someone who didn't frighten easily, that was saying a lot.

FOUR

Rachel watched a tray of canapés float by, looking shriveled and unappetizing. She had drunk a glass of champagne and considered picking another from one of the Four Seasons' white-jacketed servers.

But then, she thought, *I'll have to stay here, at this reception. And do I really want to do that?*

She thought coming to the convention would be a good idea. Stay current in her field, talk with other shrinks, and—well, she also had to admit there was the fantasy of maybe meeting someone who would make a dinner in New York the romantic fantasy that it could be.

She didn't enjoy her life alone. And she knew her daughter didn't either.

But the room was awash in balding, pudgy psychiatrists. *Surreal,* she thought. *No romance here, no one worth a dimly lit French bistro.*

A man walked up to her, a full six inches shorter than she was. "Rachel! I didn't see you."

Rachel turned. The doctor was someone she knew from San Francisco. Bumping into her at Memorial Hospital, he acted more than interested. Maybe here, with his quarry trapped, he might be feeling that he got lucky.

"I'm trying to blend in," she said.

The man sidled closer, his voice dropping conspiratorially. "I was wondering . . ." He smiled, acting like the cat that ate the canary, or vice versa. "Why don't we blow this stuffy joint. I know a place that serves the absolute best Moroccan lamb." His eyes widened. "To die for!"

Rachel looked at the elfin man. She wondered if he knew exactly how much he wasn't her fantasy. Should she tell him? Raise his consciousness? Or let him sail on, oblivious to his own lack of any real charm.

Rachel opted for sailing.

Though blowing this party was definitely the right idea.

"Sorry," Rachel said, smiling. "I'm meeting someone."

"Ohhh. I'll take a rain check."

Rachel smiled. *Take two,* she thought.

Crestfallen, the man retreated.

Rachel only wished that she *was* meeting someone.

Is there any city lonelier than New York when you're alone? I am so sick of being . . . alone.

Rachel turned and walked out to the second floor hallway of the elegant hotel. She walked down the mammoth staircase, past the austere front desk. She spied a bank of phones to her left and walked over. She could use her cellular—probably just as cheap—but old habits died hard. She picked up the pay phone.

And in a moment she heard Katherine's voice. She missed her daughter so much when she was away from her. The two of them were a team now, and Rachel felt even more alone when she was away from her Kat. She could make her laugh—even now.

"Hey sweetie, how are you?"

"Good—Mommy, I know what I want to do for my birthday!"

Rachel finally felt alive, talking to her daughter. The sound of her voice was an island of warmth in the cold business atmosphere of the lobby.

"What is that, Kat?"

"I want to go on your next trip!"

Rachel smiled. "Sounds good to me. You start your homework?"

"Yes, Mommy."

"Great." Rachel looked at the people in the lobby, some going to dinner, some checking in, some waiting for friends to arrive. She wondered: Do they have a beautiful little girl to call? Rachel felt—for the first time that night—blessed.

"Well you get ready for bed and I'll call you tomorrow."

"Okay, Mommy." A small beat. "I love you."

"Love you too, Kat. Bye."

Then, as if by magic, the connection was gone. The warmth receded. Like a fix, some quick injection that ended all too fast. Rachel stood there a second. She thought of calling Derek. But this professional junket was supposed to be a break from the Legacy, too.

So instead of calling she walked out onto Fifty-seventh Street.

Rachel walked down to Second Avenue, aimlessly wandering in that way that always made walking in New York so wonderful. At the next corner, she debated whether to head north or south. When you have no destination, it doesn't matter much.

She saw a man in an expensive-looking suit gaze at her.

Rachel looked away. *Probably thinks I'm an up-class street walker. Or do they even allow those anymore in the newly sanitized New York?*

She crossed the street, heading north.

Rob Parker sat on his rotting back porch that overlooked Hamilton harbor. The dockage of Hamilton—one of two that serviced the big cruise ships in Bermuda—was quiet. The main tourist season was over, and most of the pleasure boaters and fishermen were long gone.

And, Rob thought, *all the divers were long gone.*

He took a slug of his Red Stripe. He had a little army of the squat empty bottles lined up beside him.

Bermuda wasn't dive central. It wasn't the Bahamas, or

the Caymans, or Cozumel—all Meccas exploding with color and sea life. Enough cool water from the northern currents reached the island to make it miss the tropical explosion of colorful sea life. There were tropical fish and coral heads—but nothing divers couldn't beat by traveling another hour or so by air.

Rob took a slug of beer with the blinking lights out in the harbor his only company.

You didn't come to Bermuda for that kind of diving, Rob knew.

You came to the waters around Bermuda for wrecks. Dozens of them dotted the dive sites that girdled the gentle island. If Bermuda was a quiet jewel floating in the Atlantic, then the price for that jewel had been high—death, destruction, drowning in the vicious shallows.

Bermuda was wreck central, which was why Rob loved it. It was one thing to dive and see a big grouper going eyeball-to-eyeball with you. Quite another to float over a sunken ship that had once been crawling with life, with people. Hovering over a wreck, one could easily imagine the crew, their voices, the panic. It chilled Rob every damn time.

And there was another thing . . . new wrecks were being found all the time. The reefs and shallows extended in a crazy-quilt pattern around the island, all capable of hiding lost wrecks.

Then there were the wrecks that didn't fall victim to the vicious shallows, the ships caught by monster storms and turned upside down, and then pounded into pieces.

Wrecks were why Rob came here twenty-three years ago. Not to run a dive shop. Not to take tourists out to show them what a paddlewheel looks like after one hundred years on the bottom. Nobody knew what new wrecks could be found—and what could be found in them.

Someday, Rob knew he'd find something big. If he was patient and dived the waters, he'd find something that would change his life.

Twenty-three years ago—and he still believed.

• • •

On Seventy-Second Street, Rachel stopped at an ubiquitous Starbucks. She supposed that she should dislike the coffee chain. But the very sameness was reassuring. And the upscale Web coffeehouse dispelled any hint of late night Edward Hopper end-of-the-road loneliness.

She ordered a mocha grande . . . thinking she'd stay up late reading and sleep in tomorrow. The hell with the morning sessions. She could luxuriate in the hotel, maybe even order room service and then work off the guilt in the Four Seasons' gym.

She sat by the window watching the late night traffic on Second Avenue glide by.

The mocha tasted rich, chocolatey. *If the caffeine doesn't get me, the cocoa will.*

Another sip.

Her cell phone trilled.

She put down her coffee and dug out her Star-tac. Maybe it was Katherine, calling in with a last minute birthday idea.

Rachel looked around at the Starbucks. Nearly empty, only a pair of young lovers and an old woman sitting near the back, the employees joking around, eyeing the clock as it approached the hour of freedom.

"Hello?"

She didn't expect to hear Derek's voice. And as soon as she did, she didn't know whether to feel relieved—or afraid.

At the Luna Foundation building, Derek and the others sat around the main conference table, a satellite speakerphone sitting dead center.

Derek hated bothering Rachel. He wanted her to have some fun and get away from things.

"Rachel, can you hear me? We're all here."

Then, in order, Alex, Nick, and Philip said hello.

"Philip!" Rachel's voice came back.

She was surprised, too, Derek thought. Rachel assumed—as they all did—that it would be a long time, if ever, before they saw or heard Philip again.

"Hi, Rachel. How's New York?"

A beat. Derek guessed that she wasn't having a rollicking time. "Mighty lonely. If I can make it here . . ."

Rachel laughed a bit then. At least Derek knew that he wasn't pulling her away from some wonderful party.

"So, what's up? Why the call?"

Derek looked at Alex, who had all the material laid out in front of her.

Alex began explaining what had happened—Philip's vision, the message, the missing woman in New York—and, though possibly unrelated, Nick's attack in the sea.

Rachel interrupted. "So what are you thinking? This woman was a spirit? That she sought out Philip?"

Derek knew that Rachel struggled with the metaphysics that was a part of the struggle of the Legacy. Despite all she had seen, she wanted a rational explanation for it all.

Derek answered. "We don't know. But the coincidence is too strange to ignore."

"And Nick?" Rachel said.

"Hey, Rachel. Could be I was extraordinarily lucky."

But even as Derek heard him say the words, he knew that Nick suspected that something else was at work.

"We want you to do something, Rachel. We'll keep working out here, learning everything we can about Martina Popov. But in the meantime, we'd like you to go to her parents. Meet them. Learn about this place where Martina worked. It could be this . . . this vision of Philip's means nothing."

As soon as he said it, Derek heard the insincerity in his voice.

There was a pause. Was this something Rachel would rather not do? He looked at Alex. He supposed one of them could fly out there . . .

Then Rachel answered. "Sure. I'll go talk to them. To tell you the truth, I'm bored as hell here. The Big Apple alone isn't that much fun."

Derek smiled. "Good. Besides, I hear you can get a great borscht in Brighton."

"And the fudge at Coney Island is the best," Nick said.

On the speakerphone, Rachel laughed. "Sounds like you all wish you were here."

"Yes," Derek said. "I imagine we do. Keep in touch. And Rachel—I don't know what we're dealing with here. So be careful, okay?"

"You bet, Derek."

Derek gave her the address in Brooklyn and then the San Francisco team said good-bye.

When the call was over, they looked at each other.

"Now what?" Derek said.

"I need a bed," Nick said. "And maybe half a dozen Advil."

"I should get back to the parish," Philip said.

Derek looked at Alex. "Guess we'll keep checking the Network." He took a breath. "Something about all this worries me."

Rachel looked down at her mocha, half-full. But the plan of staying up and sleeping in was now over. She looked at the address she had just written down on her notebook. *At least this will break up the monotony,* she thought.

She got up and tossed the rest of her coffee in the trash bin.

FIVE

Jerome Farrand looked in his wallet. He had about only twenty pounds cash but he had his bank card with him, and his two credit cards. As soon as he got to an ATM he'd be fine.

He eventually moved to the footpaths that wound through the Seven Oaks region, wandering in a direction that seemed to be east until the rosy dawn confirmed the direction.

East, that's where he'd get to the village of Seven Oaks. He could find an ATM. Get some money. Then what?

He had a long walk to think over what was happening.

It was clear to him what was going on.

Last night, they came for me.

They came for me . . . because something was about to change. There was a breakthrough. And that breakthrough warranted tracking me down and eliminating me. Taking care of a loose end.

But what is that breakthrough? he wondered.

There was only one development that might warrant their finding him and killing him. There were other scholars who might recognize the signs, who might be able to see the threat.

But none as clearly as Farrand. No, the reason they tracked him down and attacked was because what he knew posed a threat to them.

He shivered in the dawn. The lush greenery to the side of the path was coated with the heavy clear dew of a foggy English morning.

He wasn't worried anymore that they were right behind him. He thanked God that he had kept up his running. Not bad for an old man. No fun getting out there and doing three miles every day. But this night . . . all that sweat had saved his life.

But what now?

First he had to figure out who to tell, who he might convince to help him. That would be the hardest part. Farrand had been ridiculed before. That was partly the reason he left the priesthood. That, and his desire to *disappear*.

But now he needed allies who might help him.

A breakthrough has occurred. A great and terrible discovery.

Yes, that was it.

And, Farrand thought, *it can only be one thing.*

More light appeared above a hillock. The village of Seven Oaks, with its Tudor-lined streets, was just ahead. So peaceful and safe.

An illusion, Farrand thought.

He picked up his pace.

Callie Peterson opened the back door to her Nyack house and let her two meowing cats inside. She watched them scurry over to their food bowls, one for each, and noisily begin devouring the crunchy food.

"Goodness, you'd think you two haven't eaten in days."

The cats paid no attention to her. Later, when they were fed, they'd amble into her studio, nestle on the table near her drawing board, her paints, her rows of colored pens and pencils.

Still in a flannel nightshirt and a cotton bathrobe, Callie

walked back to her studio, glowing with the morning light. Though the room was filled with the smell of paint, lately all her real work was done on computer. She always took to new things and when there was a better way to create her specialized art, she wasted no time getting wired.

She sat down in front of a NEC twenty-one-inch monitor. Jostling the mouse made the screen come to life. Lately she rarely shut down the machine. The computer seemed to go to sleep just fine, she thought. No need to re-start it every morning.

A small icon at the bottom of the screen showed that she was connected to her T1 line. Little icons indicated that there was a lot of mail waiting for her. But that's not what she wanted to see.

What's new . . . down there, she thought.

And she moved her mouse over the small icon of a satellite and clicked. In seconds, the screen showed a blinking array of dishes, a bunch of satellites that she could access from her quiet home in Nyack. NASA, NOAA, the U.S. Navy.

The black cat slinked into the room, mewling for attention.

"Come to visit, Inky?" Callie asked. "Well, come on then—"

Inky jumped up onto the large flat table and crouched close enough to watch Callie, but not so close as to interfere.

"Let's see what we have today."

She moved the icon over one of the satellites and clicked. Immediately she got a text message.

Downloading Current Topo Report.

Callie took a sip of her coffee. Cold already. *I really should get a Mr. Coffee in here,* she thought.

She watched while the text message blinked.

So different from the way it used to be, she thought. When she first started she had to get a hard copy of the U.S. Navy's deep ocean scans and try to piece the pages of scans together to make a map of the sea floor.

Now satellites did nearly all the work.

Very little art left. Very little imagination.

No, now the fun was elsewhere, the hunt to find some unexpected thing in the ocean. An underwater canyon here. A strange escarpment. Some unknown rolling hills half a mile under the ocean.

She didn't expect to see anything unusual . . . not where the satellite had been looking, not in the Bermuda Rise. That area was pretty well mapped.

A second cat walked in, a yellow tabby, loaded with attitude.

Callie turned to the cat. "Bored, too?"

The cat didn't answer.

Callie turned back to the screen.

The screen was filled with a topographical display of the sea floor. *Nothing unusual here,* she thought.

She moved the mouse to the left, and the map slid over. The rolling coral hummocks gave way to a flat underwater plain. It would be nice to be there this morning, Callie thought. In Bermuda, enjoying a tropical breeze and—

She stopped.

She saw something. On the sandy plain, girded by the jagged ridges of coral.

"Wait a second . . ." she said to herself.

Inky looked up at her.

"What is that?"

She increased the resolution. The image wasn't a photograph of the sea floor but a reconstruction based on electronic soundings. But those soundings could tell a lot.

Tighter on the underwater plain, until it filled the screen.

She saw the outline of something, an object sitting squarely on the sea floor. And from its shape, she guessed it wasn't natural. Not the way it sat exposed on the flat sandy bottom.

"I do believe I've found something . . ."

She moved the mouse down and opened up another program. She clicked, until a map filled the screen. This chart pinpointed the known wrecks that dotted the seas around Bermuda.

She flicked back to the satellite image, and double-checked the coordinates.

Then back to the wreck map.

She put her fingers to the screen. *Look at my hands,* she thought. *So old and wrinkled. I grew old looking at the sea floor. How did that happen?*

Her finger traced a line on the wreck map to a point in the sea . . . where there was nothing.

Nothing at all.

I've found a wreck.

An unknown wreck.

Of what, though? What ship could it be?

This . . . was fun, she thought. She'd have to tell people eventually. Let someone dive down and see what's on it.

That was for later.

It was still early.

For now, the wreck was hers.

Was it a good idea taking the subway to Brooklyn?

Maybe that was a question Rachel should have asked the Four Seasons concierge, Eduardo. But then what would Eduardo, formerly of Madrid, know of Brooklyn?

Rachel had to follow the confusing rainbow strands of the various lines to determine that the Q train would take her where she needed to go. But what should have been a quick hop to New York's seaside seemed more like a major journey.

The late morning train was filled with mothers with noisy kids, and she felt overdressed in her tan skirt and white blouse. Some of the women looked at her as though she had just beamed down from an orbiting spaceship.

Rachel smiled back at the children looking at her with big, curious eyes, missing her own Katherine—a continent away.

At first, Rachel had welcomed this assignment from Derek. But now she wasn't so sure. There was no guarantee that these people would even talk to her. And then there was a deeper question.

What am I doing in the Legacy anyway? I'm a profes-sional, she thought. *A woman of science. Not a . . . ghost-buster.*

But what had happened to her when she went back to Ireland to bury Connor and her son changed her life forever.

Did it have to be that way?

Did her life have to change?

Maybe, she thought, *I want my old life back.*

Yes, a return to naiveté. When I thought that the world was an orderly place. Not what it really is . . . not a battleground where chaos lurks, waiting.

The next stop was Newkirk Avenue, and the train emptied out. Now only a lone disheveled man of indeterminate age shared the car with her.

Not a good situation? she wondered.

The man looked over at her, his head jigging up and down with the rocking of the subway car.

He looked at her and when she looked back, he didn't look away.

Should have rented a car, she thought.

She looked away.

Looking back to the rear of the train, she could see more people in the other car. Maybe she could get up and walk to that car. Safety in numbers.

She turned back to the man.

And he was there, hanging from a strap, leaning down to her.

She sucked in a breath. He opened his mouth, displaying brownish teeth and gaps where teeth hadn't been in a long time.

" 'Scuse me, miz."

What should I do? Rachel thought. *Get up and run? And where the hell is the next stop?*

The white of the man's eyes were criss-crossed with red lines, a road map showing all the ways he'd been abusing his body.

She held her breath. The train rocked back and forth, the wheels screaming. The lights flickered out. Then on again, then out.

"I was . . . won'erin . . ."

Rachel looked to the other end of the car. *Get up,* she thought, *and run to the next car.*

"But . . ." the man smiled, a hideous grimace, "you look lost. Could I help you some?"

He stood there, dangling like a piece of human meat from the strap.

Rachel shook her head. She managed a smile.

"No. I'm fine. I know where I'm going."

The man's smile faded. He looked at her as though he didn't quite believe her. Then he stood erect, pulled back from Rachel, and walked back to his seat.

On cue, the next station reared into view.

King's Highway.

She unfolded the subway map in her purse.

Two more stops, and she'd be at Brighton Beach.

Last exit in Brooklyn, she saw.

Good title for a book.

The train stopped. No one got on.

Philip walked back out to the altar. The seven A.M. Mass was over, and all the good people who came to start their day with the sacrament of the Eucharist were gone.

Philip glanced out at the pews. Not everyone was gone. He saw an old lady in the front, kneeling, rosaries in hand, her lips moving a mile a minute. Philip nodded and smiled at her.

Pray for us all, he thought. He wondered if such people, the silent ones that prayed so hard, helped charge up humanity's battery against evil. Could the good intentions of a few help us all?

And in the back, he saw a man in the shadows. Maybe a businessman stopping for a quick prayer. Philip didn't remember seeing anyone like that at the early Mass.

Sitting way back in the shadows . . . Praying for who knows what.

Philip walked up to the altar and removed the white cloth from the altar table. He folded it neatly, then genuflected.

Another glance into the pews. The woman, her eyes shut, still praying so hard.

Philip walked back into the sacristy.

Today would be a busy day. Hospital visits. A CYO basketball game this afternoon. Adult confirmation classes in the evening. But it was a day doing what Philip wanted to do, serving people, dealing with the matters of faith and hope that meant so much to him.

He tried not to think of the girl, of his vision from the other day.

Right, he thought, putting the folded cloth in a cabinet, *and try not to think of a pink elephant.*

He looked around. The sacristy was cleaned up, wine and cruets put away, he was almost ready to leave.

Last thing he had to do was snuff out the candles.

He grabbed the long-necked candle snuffer and walked back to the church.

The old woman was gone. He extinguished the candles on the left side of the altar, just below a statue of the Virgin Mother, and then crossed to the other side, genuflecting at the midpoint. When he stood up, he turned around.

The lone figure, the man, still kneeled in the back.

Philip wondered if he should go talk to him.

A man kneeling there, so long, praying. Could be he has some big problem. He might need someone to talk to.

Philip extinguished the other candles. Sleepy smoke rose from the wicks, this time curling by the plaster feet of a statue of St. Joseph.

Philip turned around.

The man was still there.

Sure, I should talk to him, he thought.

Philip walked to the altar rail and opened it. The noisy click of the bolt echoed in the cavernous church.

He left the railing gate open and walked down the aisle.

So dark, back there. A gloomy place to seek solace, he thought.

His shoes made a squeaking noise on the polished floor.

Close to the rear of the church, the man still sat in the shadows.

Closer, and Philip saw that the man's eyes were closed. He was bald and wore a suit. His skin looked tight on his face. Not the usual customer at St. Pat's, Philip thought. The church didn't get too many businessmen.

Maybe—

Philip hesitated.

Maybe I should just let him be.

But if the man needs someone to talk to, I should reach out.

"Excuse me," Philip said quietly. Though just above a whisper, his voice sounded eerily loud in the empty building.

"Sir, is there anything I can do . . . for you?"

The man didn't move.

His eyes locked shut.

Was he asleep, Philip wondered?

"Could I help you?"

Still no answer. *Maybe I should just leave him alone.*

Give the man some peace.

But for some reason, Philip felt that he wanted to touch the man's shoulder. Make sure that he had been heard, that his offer of someone to talk to had been heard . . .

He touched the man's shoulder.

The man moved his head. He turned to Philip. Eyes shut. Now Philip noticed something about the man. How his bald head, the tight skin, the chiseled cut of his jaw, seemed somehow . . . not quite human.

He put out his hand. Covered Philip's hand.

Philip looked down at the hand. Only, in the dim light, where he expected to see skin, a hand, fingers . . . he felt the fingers dig into his hand.

Except they weren't fingers.

The hand was a claw, with only three appendages curled tight around Philip's hand.

Philip pulled back, but the claw hand held him.

He looked up to the man's face.

The man's eyes were now open. Twin black pools, each cut with a thin crimson strip. The claw hand tightened.

The man tilted his head and opened his mouth.

And Philip looked at that mouth. *I don't want to see*

56

what's there, he thought. *This is just another vision, just another hallucination. I can simply close my eyes and make it vanish.*

He blinked.

The claw hand tightened. The mouth opened showing no teeth, but a gaping hole, more like the sucking mouth of some lizard or reptile.

Philip heard moans. A pathetic, terrified sound.

Coming from his own mouth.

He looked down at the claw hand digging into his flesh, the claws like nails, digging deep. Even in the darkness, the stream of blood glistened.

This isn't real, Philip told himself. *It's just another vision, an illusion.*

But every sense screamed that it was real.

Someone came up behind him.

Then, a voice—

"Father, Father—is—"

Philip turned. The old woman. Still holding the rosary.

"Is everything—"

The woman. A parishioner. What was she seeing?

"Oh, God," she cried.

Philip looked at her, now even more horrified. She could see. She saw . . . all this.

The man turned to her and hissed.

"Father!" the woman said. And she pressed the rosary into Philip's free hand. Philip grabbed the ancient string of beads and then took the crucifix and touched the claw hand imprisoning him. As if burnt, the hand recoiled. Then Philip pressed the cross against the leathery skin of the man's forehead.

And from that man's gaping mouth escaped the sound of an animal being cut. The deep horrible groan filled the church.

The man stood up.

The woman behind Philip prayed, aloud now. Our Father quickly cascaded into Hail Mary, ever faster.

Philip's hand holding the rosary shook. But he held it in front of him, while he took a step closer.

He searched his mind for words.

"By the power of our Lord, leave—"

He took a breath . . .

"Leave this hallowed place. By the loving power—"

The man leapt up to the seat of the pew. The black eyes blinked, the slits narrowed. The toothless mouth spoke . . .

"We await you, stupid priest."

The creature stretched out its claw hand and shot straight up, grasping the railing of the choir loft above. Philip watched it slither over the railing, incongruous in its lizard-like movements, clothed in a suit.

Philip watched.

Stood there, bleeding, shaking.

The old woman wrapped her scarf around his hand. She kept praying, her voice calm, steady, her faith her rock, her protection.

He looked at her. He should be comforting her, reassuring her, praying for her.

"Thank you," he said.

The woman didn't stop though, just nodded, tightening the makeshift bandage as she prayed.

SIX

After Farrand got some money from the ATM near the train station in Seven Oaks, he went to the newsstand and scanned the local paper to see if the headlines mentioned anything about what happened the night before.

There was nothing. *Just as well,* he thought. That would make it easier for him to travel.

The rail trip to London through the gentle countryside was a soothing backdrop to the chaotic jumble of his thoughts.

By the time he got to London it was afternoon and he wasn't even sure he'd get to see the person he wanted to.

The Jesuits maintained an administrative building in Bloomsbury, nestled among the literary agents and bankers. The four-story building was, Farrand once was told, a Catholic bulwark against the absurdities of Anglicanism.

Farrand hesitated outside the door.

He felt like a kid coming home after some crazy spree.

And he thought . . . *how do I look? I need a shave. That's for sure. My clothes look like hell. They thought I was crazy when I left. What ever will they think now?*

He walked up the stone steps of 21 Hamersmith Row, to the giant polished oak door. The doorbell was nestled in a gleaming golden fixture. Farrand took a breath and pressed the button.

Rachel looked around at the street signs. There was Surf Avenue, but where was Bay Street? She would have asked someone but Brighton Beach seemed like a ghost town.

She looked out at the ocean, dark, gray, churning. She watched a nearby swell send a foamy spit of white surf flying above the rocky shore.

I should have picked up a map, she thought.

Just then she spotted someone walking toward her, a young man in jeans and a workshirt. Rachel waited on the corner for the man to get close.

"Excuse me, but do you—"

The young man stopped and tilted his head.

"I'm trying to find . . . Bay Street?"

The man smiled, and then said something that Rachel assumed was Russian. Rachel smiled. Welcome to Little Russia.

"Bay . . . Street," she said slowly.

A light bulb went on. The man smiled. "Bay Street? Da." He then proceeded to give Rachel some directions in a mix of Russian and gesture, dotted with the occasional English words "go" and "yes?". Rachel smiled and thanked the man. At least she had enough to find the street, and the home of the Popovs.

She looked out at the ocean, so close and threatening. It was almost as though this small enclave was a guardian, keeping the ocean from racing toward Manhattan, eager to tear down the skyscrapers.

Rachel hurried toward Bay Street.

Nick lay in bed, reading. He felt beat, exhausted by the dive, the attack . . . the weirdness. The Legacy might need him—but for now he needed some peace and quiet.

From his apartment he could see the Presidio, its fortress-like walls visible even in the morning fog that didn't seem to want to burn off.

He flipped the pages of a book on D day, Stephen Ambrose's *Citizen Soldier*. *There's no way we can really connect to that experience,* he thought. *No way we can imagine what it's like to sit inside a landing craft and get dumped into hell.*

Kind of puts my life in perspective, Nick thought.

Nothing he ever did as a SEAL, even the explosives work during the Gulf War, came even close.

Not even his work with the Legacy.

And he thought, *Is that what attracts me to the Legacy, this sense of a great mission, fighting an enemy when the stakes are so big?*

Is it all about my ego?

He reached over to grab the container of Advil. The slight turn made him feel the wounds. Could've been a lot worse. The shark serrated his skin but that was about it. The tiger's jaw could easily have cracked some ribs.

Is this . . . all I want from my life? he thought.

What about what everyone else dreams about? A house, a wife, kids. Barbecue in the backyard. A beer or two with some friends. A round of golf.

What is my life all about? Demons . . . damnation . . . the fate of the world.

Sounds big enough.

He leaned back, pressing his head into the too-soft pillow.

He should get up. Walk around a bit. Maybe go over to see Derek and Alex.

He closed his eyes.

It felt so nice . . .

He fell asleep.

Derek came back from his morning run and saw Alex's car parked out front.

She's great, he thought. *Always dependable, never questioning what it is we do. Never questioning the demands I make.*

Derek entered the key code and went into the building.

He didn't see Alex on the ground floor, which meant that she was already at her computer terminal. Derek went into he kitchen, fixed two cups of coffee, put them on a tray, and carried them upstairs.

He saw Alex sitting close to her monitor, her face catching the blue glow of the screen.

Derek put the coffee down near her.

"Oh, I didn't hear you come in."

"I was in stealth mode. You're here early."

Alex nodded. "Yes. Something bothered me all night." She turned to Derek. He took a sip of his coffee.

"I've been thinking too."

"It's something my mother once said, an island expression. She used to say to me . . . that all winds come from somewhere . . . and go somewhere."

"Hard to argue with that logic."

"Well, what it meant was that that things happen for a reason, that there are hidden forces at work, like a wind that can blow us one way or the other."

Derek sat down. Of all the members of the Legacy, Alex was perhaps the most gifted. She could also be the most rational, the most scientific—even while dealing with the most irrational material.

But if she had feelings, Derek wanted to know what they were.

"Go on."

"I was thinking about Philip's vision. Why him? Whatever it was—and we don't know where it came from— why Phil? And then, maybe even occurring at the same time, Nick got attacked . . ."

"And saved."

"Yes. And later I want to show you some of the material I've found on animal attacks, the symbolism of those attacks. Some strange stuff. But these two events . . . I think they're linked."

"Nick's dive and Philip's vision, linked?"

"Yes. Extraordinary things happen to two members of

62

the Legacy. And they, in turn, set in motion another member, Rachel."

"Something about this . . . this 'wind' bothers you?"

"Yes. I lay awake last night. I was almost waiting for something to happen to me. Or you. But I feel that this isn't a normal event that the Legacy investigates."

"I didn't know there was such a thing for us. Normal? the Legacy? They don't seem to go together."

Alex stood up. "No. That's not what I mean. Every time we get involved, we investigate something that we discovered, something pointing to some evil. But this time—it's as though something is reaching out to us."

Derek nodded. He had been having some of the same thoughts. But he didn't want to color Alex's view. "Yes, you're right. I've been thinking that too. This time, something may be reaching out to the Legacy—though I'm not convinced that Nick and Philip's incidents are related."

Alex walked close to him. "I am. I think they're connected. And there's one more thing, Derek . . ."

"Yes."

If something is reaching out to us, we don't know what—or why."

Another sip of coffee. Derek looked around at the bank of computers, this high-tech room wired to the world above and its secret underground network. There would be no answers to that big question here.

The phone rang and Alex jumped. Derek watched her.

"God, Philip! No . . . where are you?"

Derek took a step closer.

It could only mean one thing.

More. Another attack. And now they were all in danger.

Alex hit a button, and suddenly Philip was on speakerphone.

2555 Bay Street wasn't a small house. Though most of the homes on this block in Brighton Beach were little two-story houses with aluminum siding and narrow peaked roofs, this house was a full story taller, with massive columns in front.

Apparently the Popovs knocked down whatever was here

and built something that looked like a pocket mansion.

Rachel rang the bell. No telling if someone would be home. But she didn't want to risk the family telling her to stay away.

The air had turned cool, with a hint of dampness. *Should have listened to the weather report,* she thought. *I'll probably get soaked walking back to the subway.*

She rang the bell again.

Rachel thought she heard movement from behind the door.

Rachel smiled at the small view hole.

The door opened an inch, held back by a chain.

"Yes," a man said, his accented voice deep.

"Mr. Popov? Hello."

Now came the hard part. Getting the man to talk to her.

"Who are you? We're not buying anything," he said in a thick accent.

Rachel kept the smile on her face. "I'm not selling anything, Mr. Popov. I'm here about your daughter."

Suddenly the man's face was in the narrow opening. "Who are you? Are you police? I've spoken to all the police! Have you found—".

"No, Mr. Popov. I'm not from the police. I'm from somewhere else. And I think I know something . . . about your daughter." It was a lie, but she needed to get inside.

Rachel dug in her purse and took out her California MD identification. "I'm a psychiatrist, a doctor. Can I come in? For a bit and—"

"Mikhail, who is it?"

Another voice. Mrs. Popov?

"It's a doctor, Laina. She says she knows something about Martina."

"Yes? She knows something?" The woman's voice was closer.

God, what do I know, Rachel thought? *I'm really here to learn about their daughter. I have nothing to give them.*

"Let her in, Mikhail. Open the door!"

Mr. Popov looked out at Rachel. His eyes, dark and rheumy, were filled with suspicion, pain . . .

The door shut. Rachel heard the latch being slipped off. And then the door reopened.

SEVEN

Farrand waited in the luxurious library. The bloodred carpet seemed almost garish surrounded by the somber heavy oak bookshelves. An austere couch faced two equally plain chairs. Beveled windows let in light but no images from the street.

Farrand didn't sit.

He tried to think how he would begin and how he would explain why he was here.

I should have found a rest room, he thought. *Some place to wash my face, smooth my hair. I must look . . . bizarre.*

This waiting seemed interminable, the room nearly suffocating.

Farrand wanted to open one of the windows. He reached out and touched the sliding pole latch that opened the window. A small round nut at one end was screwed down tight. *Maybe I could just loosen it,* he thought. *Let some air in.*

He touched the nut and gave it a small turn to see if anyone had used it lately.

I must look crazy, he thought. *A crazy old man.*

The door to the library opened. A tall, chunky priest with

a head of curly gray hair, wire frame glasses, and a ruddy complexion walked in.

"Jerry," the priest said.

Farrand smiled. "Tom. Thank you. For seeing me."

The priest nodded. "I'd always make time for one of my mentors. Can I get you something? Some tea. A glass of wine?"

Farrand felt the younger priest looking him over. If he was shocked—and he probably was—Tom Murray was doing a good job of hiding it.

"No, nothing." Farrand looked down at the chairs and the couch. "Can we sit? I need . . . well, I need to talk to you."

"Right. Should I get a pad?. Take some notes?"

Farrand nodded. *Yes . . . take down all the crazy things I say.*

Murray walked over to a small secretary by the entrance, opened a drawer, and took out a yellow pad. He came back and took one of the chairs.

"Have a seat, Jerry." The priest looked right at Farrand. Then he smiled. "You know, you look like you've been up all night. Out late partying?"

Farrand smiled. He looked at the priest who he once taught decades ago, back when he was a priest. He looked at his black cassock, the stiff white collar—the emblems of the power the church represented.

How will he react to what I say, he thought?

"You sure you don't want a cup of something? Maybe some nice biscuits? The cook does—"

Farrand held up a hand. It was late in the day. One day gone, and who knew how many left.

"I'd best start, Tom. Tell you what happened last night. Then tell you something that you might not know . . . unless they decided that they wanted it all in my file."

The priest shrugged. "I haven't checked anything . . ."

"No matter—I'll tell you it all. Starting last night."

Farrand looked toward the windows. The light had noticeably faded. *A cloudy day darkens that much more quickly,* he thought. He wished it would stay light forever.

"Something happened last night? To you?"

Farrand nodded.

He rubbed his chin, feeling the day's growth of beard. *I look like a homeless person,* he thought. *Or the demented ancient mariner with my crazed tale.*

How crazed? How demented?

Farrand was sure that what he was about to tell the priest would—as they say—be off the charts.

Nick slept. And he knew he was dreaming. Though in his dreams he wasn't really sure if it was night or day, whether this was a nap or a full night's sleep. He didn't have that much awareness.

But he knew he was dreaming.

At first, he was back at the dive.

Only this time there was no escaping the tiger shark. He kicked as hard as he could but whenever he looked back through the clear blue water, the shark was there, following him.

Then it hit, pulling at his leg. Then the shark attacked his other leg. In his dream the blue water quickly turned a filmy red. In his dream, there were no hammerheads to circle and protect him.

The red, filmy water filled his dream as the dull thud of shark hits became a tattoo, beating on him, without pain as if he was just a dull observer watching it all happen.

Until it stopped.

He knew it was a dream. Just a bad dream.

Sleeping, he tried to concentrate on that fact.

He opened his eyes.

His mouth was dry. The bandages on his back stung. The pillow was wet. He looked out his window, unable to tell what time it was.

At least he was awake. Bad enough living through that attack once. *I don't need any replays in my dreams,* he thought. *So thirsty. Got to get up and get something to drink.*

He heard the sounds of cars beeping outside. He looked at the television. *Put it on,* he thought. *Fill the room with*

68

some mindless chatter. A soap. A game show. CNN. Anything.

He clicked the ON button on the remote. Nothing happened.

Again.

It must need batteries, he thought.

He walked over to the small TV and pressed the ON button. But nothing happened.

Strange, he thought.

His dry tongue again snaked out and grazed his parched lips. *God, so thirsty.*

He walked into the kitchen. The dingy white curtains masked most of the light. The small digital clock on top of the counters read 12:30. *Only slept a few hours,* he thought.

Nothing really.

I would have liked to sleep away this day. Then get back to Derek and the others tomorrow. See what help I—

He opened the cupboard.

And heard movement. From behind.

He turned. Listened. Frozen into that attentive position when something not right enters the sensory environment.

The "what was that" response.

He turned into a living statue, frozen. There was no other sound. He saw that his bag of garbage was nearly full. *Should empty that,* Nick thought.

He reached up and grabbed a glass.

He turned on the water. It coughed for a second and then he filled his glass. Good old SF tap water. He chugged one glass, then refilled it and chugged another.

And while he was gulping. He heard the noise again. He turned around.

The garbage bag had toppled over. He walked over to the bag, now spewing a banana peel, an orange juice container, and a nice splash of coffee grinds onto the floor.

"Shit," Nick said.

He bent down to pick up the mess.

How did it just fall? he wondered.

He righted the bag and scooped up as much of the mess as he could with his bare hands. Bending down like this made his wounds ache. He imagined the cuts opening, starting to bleed again. Soon his hands were dotted with the coffee grinds.

He went to the sink and turned on the faucet with his elbow, like a doctor scrubbing up. He rinsed off the grinds and then grabbed a wad of paper towels, wet them, and mopped up the remains.

I should just go back to bed . . .

Then . . . amidst the grinds, he saw something else, something encrusted with the grinds that he couldn't identify, oval clumps of . . . something.

Not about to inspect it now, he thought.

He stuffed the towel wad into the too-full garbage bag.

He refilled his water glass and walked back into his bedroom. The bed looked so attractive. But then he saw the TV. Electricity was still on. Everything in the kitchen was fine. So what the hell was the problem with the stupid TV set?

He walked over to it and hit the power button a few more times, and nothing happened. Is it unplugged, he thought?

Nick looked behind the set, at the wall socket. Nope, all plugged in—

But . . .

The electrical cord was cut.

"What?" Nick said. He picked up the cord and, about midway between the set, it looked sawed off at an angle. He looked at the other end. *That's live electricity,* he thought, *110 volts live.*

He gingerly reached past it and yanked the cord out of its socket.

Then he reexamined the cut end. What did this? Did someone come in here, cut the cord?

Yeah, right. That was likely to happen.

He looked around the room. The only thing he wanted to do now was go to sleep.

He walked over to his bed and fell into it. *Let me sleep until tomorrow,* he thought. *Let me—*

He felt something.

Something move.

Under the covers.

The air turned icy. He froze . . . but then he felt the movement again . . . near his feet. Under the covers.

I'm losing it, he thought. *Nothing could be moving. I'm just losing it.*

Then against the telltale rustle of blanket and sheet, the feeling of something coming closer.

Something brushed his foot. Fur. Then something . . . slithery.

Nick leaped out of bed, stumbling to the floor, landing on . . . more of these black things he saw in the coffee grinds. He held up his hand, seeing these black raisinlike things stuck to the palm of his hand, squashed flat. His breathing was ragged, panicked.

Another sound from the kitchen. The garbage falling over again.

He stood up. He reached out and grabbed the bedsheets. With a giant sweep he tossed them back.

The exposed rat looked around.

It had chewed a hole into the mattress, a little crater. Pausing only a second, it started to chew again.

Nick stepped back.

He heard squeaks . . . from the kitchen.

The rat on the bed was big, the size of a cat. Nick felt as if he could throw up. He looked at the TV. The cut wire . . . hadn't been cut. No, the rat had chewed it.

In bare feet, Nick walked to the kitchen.

The garbage was again sideways on the floor, but now a big brown-gray rat sat on top of the bag, and then another squiggled out of the side of the bag covered with a mixture of sodden garbage.

All of sudden his apartment was infested with rats.

Something moved across his bare foot.

A smaller rat crawled over his foot, its snakelike tail trailing.

Got to get someone, Nick thought. *This is sick.* He started for the hallway door, passing his closet where—he heard a sound inside. Lots of sounds. As if he might open the closet door and see the small closet filled with rats.

Nick grabbed the doorknob to the front door to the hallway.

He pulled open the door to see the hallway filled with rats, crawling over each other, looking expectantly.

No fucking way, Nick thought. *I've got to get out of here.*

He started walking down the hallway. A few rats moved aside as he stepped onto the cold stone floor. But then one rat, a dusky grayish-brown came up and nipped at his big toe. Nick kicked at it, and the fat rodent made an annoyed whelp. Nick kept moving, his stomach heaving, and now if a rat came close, he kicked at it.

The stairs were ahead.

Another rat came close, its mouth open and its incisors ready. It tried to bite Nick as he kicked at it but Nick caught the animal in its soft belly. The creature rolled away.

The rats seemed to give up the idea of nipping him.

He walked through the living minefield.

To the stairs.

Hoping to God that the stairs down were not also filled with rats.

He got to the top of the staircase, and saw that they were free.

Nick hurried down the stairs hoping that what he saw . . . had really happened, that he wasn't losing his mind.

And as he walked down, he left behind a small trail of blood smearing the steps all the way down the two flights.

EIGHT

Rachel sat in the tiny living room. Matreshkas sat on the mantel, bearded priests and bears and women in babushkas, all hiding other nested figures. *Kind of a nice metaphor for one's mind,* she thought. Personality nested into personality. There were also two photos, portraits, Martina on one side, and a man on the other. A son, she guessed.

The woman, Mrs. Popov, looked like a typical Russian peasant. Her giant breasts were barely encased in a simple dress, and her hair was not so much cut as hedged. Mikhail Popov was an imposing figure, tall with a silvery gray beard and hair, sparkling blue eyes. A handsome, strong-looking man.

The woman poured Rachel a cup of tea.

The father sat in a giant easy chair that easily took up a quarter of the space in the room.

"So . . . what is it you do with the police?"

Laina Popov sat on the sofa. Rachel saw that she had a handkerchief in her hand, wound into the warp and weft of her fingers.

Rachel smiled. "I'm not with the police. I'm a psychiatrist—"

The man looked at his wife. Psychiatrist was obviously a bad word.

"Not with the police . . . then what are you doing here?"

Rachel tried to gauge how she should do this. The truth would likely be too much.

"I specialize in people who . . . unusual things have happened to . . ."

"Unusual? My daughter disappears . . . maybe killed and—"

His wife started crying.

"Mamushka!" he said. A rebuke. Rachel took an immediate dislike to the man. He may have escaped Mother Russia and made a life here, but still this was the next millennium. That wifely subservient crap belonged in the Dumpster. Period.

"A disappearance like this . . . it's not normal. I don't know what the police told you—"

"They told me that they had special teams 'investigating'!" His voice dripped with contempt. She guessed where he came from the police weren't exactly trusted allies.

"Yes," Rachel said feeding into his contempt. "That's why I thought I'd come—" She handed him her card. Popov looked at it.

"California? You came all the way from California!"

Rachel shook her head. "No. I mean, I did—but not for this. I'm here for a big convention. I saw your story. I thought I might help."

The old woman cleared her throat. The husband glared—but then he seemed to soften. Maybe the bear's bark was worse than his bite.

"You'd like to help?" the woman said. "That might be . . . good. But tell me . . . how can you help us?"

"I'm not too sure. But if you tell me about your daughter, her life, her coworkers, there might be something there. Of course, if I learn anything I will tell the police . . ."

Another lie.

The police might be the last people she would tell.

"Yes, okay then. I'll tell you about our girl, our wonderful Martina. And maybe . . . maybe . . ." the man's voice began to break ". . . you can help us find her."

Martina Popov, Rachel learned, worked for an antiquities gallery in SoHo, near the intersection of Spring and Sullivan, a very trendy area. Rachel knew the area well. Every time she came to Manhattan she made a point of trolling the too-hip boutiques and trying out the newest bistros and subterranean restaurants.

Martina's title, her father told Rachel proudly, was Assistant to the Director at Okthoro Gallery & Antiquities. From what she could glean from Mr. Popov, it was both a gallery and a specialized dealer in rare antiquities. Martina was an expert in Ancient Egypt, with a masters from Columbia University.

"With a full scholarship!" Mr. Popov said proudly.

And Martina loved her job, loved the great city, and loved the people she worked with. She had progressed in the company, even making trips to Egypt on behalf of the gallery.

"But no romance," Mrs. Popov added. Rachel heard the concern in the woman's voice. Forget everything else . . . it was the ring on the left hand that was important.

"No. But she was happy. Enjoying her work. But then—" The father stopped.

"Things changed."

Another look at the mother, and Rachel began to suspect the real power in this family lay with the woman twisting the handkerchief in her hands.

"Martina grew quiet . . ."

"But it was more than that," Mrs. Popov added.

"Yes. She no longer smiled, she seemed worried, filled with troubles. In Russia we had a saying. The clouds have gathered. And they didn't go away."

"Did you try talking to her?"

Mr. Popov looked away. Rachel imagined that talking about things didn't come too easily to this man. She was almost tempted to tell the man about Philip's vision, that he saw his daughter, heard her a continent away.

They have enough to worry about, she decided.

Mrs. Popov spoke.

"I did. One night . . . it was so late. And Martina was in our kitchen, sitting with a glass of wine. And I could see, under those lights, how scared she looked. So I sat down. I—I—" The woman started to crack. More fussing with her handkerchief. "I asked her—she was my baby. I asked her what was wrong. And I never forget how she looked at me. Her beautiful dark eyes ready to cry. But more than that. She said to me, "Mama, I think the people are doing something very wrong.""

"Very wrong?" Rachel asked. "Did she—"

The woman shook her head. "I asked, but no. She said . . . she might have to leave the gallery. Might try to leave."

The word "try" hung in the room.

"That—" Mikhail Popov said, "was three weeks ago. There were more late nights."

"But no more talks?" Rachel looked at Martina's mother. She shook her head.

The two people were upset. *And,* thought Rachel, *maybe this was enough for now.* She could check out the Okthoro gallery.

Rachel took out a small pad. "Here's my number at the hotel. I want to talk to some other people." She handed Mr. Popov the piece of paper. "Maybe we can talk later?"

Mr. Popov made a slight nod. No commitment there. But the door was open.

Rachel stood up. "Thank you."

Mrs. Popov took Rachel's hand and squeezed. "Please. Help us. I—I love my daughter so much . . ."

And with that the two people both started crying as if they were alone with their loss and their pain.

Back at the Four Seasons, Rachel sat on the bed and leafed through the yellow pages. She found the listing for Okthoro Antiquities. Perhaps she could go down there tonight. SoHo tended to stay open late.

But she heard a sharp knock on the door. Maids coming to turn down the bed? A bit early for that . . .

She opened the door. A tall, dark-haired man, about thirty-two, stood there, dressed in a gray suit. He was handsome in a severe way, the lines of his jaw chiseled . . . and he wasn't smiling.

"Yes?"

"Rachel Corrigan?"

The man's eyes were black. She recognized him then, even as he said his name.

"I'm Gregor Popov. Can I come in?"

It wasn't really a question.

And Rachel thought, *I invaded his family's privacy. This visit was to be expected.*

"Er, sure, I—" He stepped into the room and shut the door behind him.

"You went to my parents' house?"

"Yes, I—"

"Listen, I don't know who you are, whether you're even a psychiatrist. But you are to leave my parents alone! Do you understand?"

"I was only trying—am trying—to help. If you'll—"

He seemed ready to leave. "If you so much as knock on their door, I'll call the cops." He shook his head. "What kind of nut are you?"

She was done here, Rachel knew, unless she did something.

She went to one of the end tables and grabbed a hotel pen and small pad. She wrote down a number, ripped it off the pad, and handed it to Gregor Popov.

"There. Call that number."

"What is this?"

"San Francisco Memorial Hospital. I have psychiatric privileges at the hospital. I'm not a nut. And, God, all I want to do is help your parents, your sister."

Greg looked at the piece of paper.

"Call it. They'll tell you who I am. And downstairs, in the meeting rooms, believe it or not, I know hundreds of psychiatrists from around the country."

He looked up and held her eyes with his gaze. "So you're a bona fide shrink? That doesn't give you the right to bother my parents."

What could she do? She had no choice. She had to tell him the truth. But not just about Philip's vision, and Martina, and the Legacy. But back further, about her husband, and how she got involved in this insanity to begin with.

"Can you listen a bit?"

"Sure."

She smiled. "Then shut the door and take a seat. Because I'm not sure what you're going to think after you hear this . . ."

And she started by talking about the day she and Katherine, her sweet daughter, visited Connor's grave in Ireland, where it all began.

She finished.

Greg handed her back the photos . . . of Connor first, then Katherine.

"She's very cute," he said.

"Kat's my life," Rachel said.

"But your story . . . I don't know. I'm sorry, but it's all too fantastic. There's no way I can believe much of it, or any of it." He smiled. For the first time. And Rachel smiled back.

"Okay. I know it's fantastic. But even if it all means nothing, the visions, anything . . . strange. Your sister is still missing. And I'd like to help."

Greg looked at her. "What were you going to do?"

"I was going to go to this SoHo gallery where your sister worked. Try to see if I can learn anything there, who were her friends, what she did . . ."

Greg's expression changed. "She used to talk about her work a lot—at first. Very excited. She even did some trips to Cairo for them. But in the past few months . . . well, I left messages and she didn't return them. I guess I thought she was just partying."

"Your parents said the same thing."

"You know, I don't believe any of this you've told me.

78

But I do believe that you are—for some reason—concerned about my sister. Maybe I could help you. We could go to the gallery together. Ask some questions."

Rachel stood up. "That sounds great. How about you give me ten minutes to freshen up. And we'll go down to SoHo."

"Great. I'll meet you in the lobby."

"See you in ten."

And Gregor stood up and walked out the door.

Rachel stood there for a second. *I have an ally,* she thought. *Probably a good thing to have in this city. Probably a good thing to have when you don't have a damn clue what you're facing.*

She needed to hurry. But first, she wanted to call Derek before she went to SoHo and let him know her plan.

Rachel and Greg stood outside the gallery on Spring Street.

"Looks closed," Greg said. "I thought you said that it was open late?"

"I called . . . but—" Rachel leaned close. "God!"

What is it?"

"It's Monday. And the gallery is closed on Monday."

It was five P.M., and the old streets of SoHo, some with the original cobblestones exposed, were filled with people racing home. Rachel looked at Greg. "I'm sorry, it just must not have registered. Brought you all the way down here for nothing."

Greg looked around at the sea of people, the young, the hip, and those desperate to appear so.

"As long as we're here, why waste the trip?"

"What?"

"Feel like dinner?"

"Sure."

Greg smiled. "Ever try Balthazar? Great for celebrity spotting, French bread and oysters."

"Oysters?" Rachel said smiling.

Greg looked embarrassed. "Oh, sorry—forgot the dreaded oyster potency cliché." His smile broadened. "I just like them because they taste so yummy."

"Sure you do," Rachel laughed. "To Balthazar then?"
And she took Greg's arm.

They sat in a back booth, two plates of oysters all gone,
and a half-finished pile of frites on the table. The bottle of
Beaujolais Villages 1996 was almost gone too. They had
moved past the small talk stage and were sharing what Rachel called the "real stuff."

Greg poured the last of the wine into her glass. "Another
bottle?" he said.

She shook her head. "I've already had my fill. It's very
good and—" she looked around at the newly minted art
deco look of the restaurant "—I *love* this place."

"I saw Scorcese here one night," Greg said. "And the
artist Peter Beard. And it's always filled with models."

"Hence your regular visits."

Greg smiled at her teasing jibe. "I like the bread."

"And the oysters."

Greg held the smile . . . but then let it fade. He leaned
across the table, closer to her.

"I've been thinking about what you've told me. About
this group you work for, and how this priest saw my sister."

He looked around as if worried that someone might hear
him. "Now that I know you, I can't imagine that you'd get
mixed up in something so wacky, so 'out-there.' Unless—"

Another look around.

"Go on."

"Unless it was true. Unless everything you told me is
true."

"Remember, Greg, that I said we don't know what's going on. That's one reason I wanted to speak with your parents—"

"I know. You—we—don't know anything. But now that
I know you, now that I can believe you even a bit, I'm
scared."

Rachel nodded. "And you should be, Greg. If something
dark, something strange, has happened to your sister, then
she's reaching out to us. And we don't know why."

"It's too freaky."

The waiter, wearing the giant apron of a Parisian garçon, appeared by the table. "Coffee?" he asked.

Greg looked at Rachel.

"Do you have to run?"

She shook her head.

"Some coffee would be nice."

"Two, please." The waiter nodded and wheeled away.

"Tell me, Rachel—"

"Yes?"

"This could be dangerous?"

She nodded. "More than you can imagine. Especially considering how little we know. But Greg—there's also the possibility that everything will have a perfectly normal explanation."

The words sounded false.

"But if not—not only my sister could get hurt?"

Rachel nodded.

"There could be danger to you, to me, to my parents."

"I can't lie, Greg. What the Legacy faces is deadly. That's why if you want to back away, I'll understand perfectly."

"I'm in for the duration, understand?"

"Great. You know, I was getting kind of lonely in this big city."

The waiter brought the two coffees and a jar of synthetic sweeteners and chunks of brown sugar.

Later, they stood together outside the Four Seasons.

"Nice digs," he said.

"It's where they're having the conference."

"And it has a smashing bar."

"Is that an invitation?" Rachel asked.

Greg looked at his watch. "I wish it could be. But I have a court date at nine A.M. and miles more paper to read over."

Rachel tried to hide the disappointment.

"But let me meet you in the afternoon, and we'll go back to the gallery, okay?"

"Sounds great."

And I'll even scout another great place for dinner. That is . . ."

"I'd love to."

Then, quite unexpectedly, Greg leaned close and kissed her on each cheek.

"A Russian good-bye," he said. "Until tomorrow."

"See you then," Rachel said and she entered the elegant hotel lobby not feeling sleepy at all.

"What do you want me to do?" Father Murray said.

Farrand looked outside. It was late. The London restaurants and pubs were full, so much life outside. Everything seemed so out of focus, sitting in this richly decorated room. The night before, the attack, all seemed a light year away.

Maybe I imagined it all.

Farrand spoke quietly. "Do you have a TV in this room?"

"Yes. Why?"

"Could you put on the nine o'clock news?"

Father Murray walked over to a giant mahogany armoire and opened it, revealing the TV. He picked up the remote and the TV came on.

The news was beginning.

"What are you looking for?"

Farrand held up a hand, silencing the other priest.

The camera went from a shot of the whole news set to a close-up of young woman reporter.

"This is important?" The priest said.

"Listen . . . please . . ."

The woman spoke. "This evening, there's terrible news from the Seven Oaks area of Kent. A family was brutally murdered last night. Three bodies were found, but a fourth person, a tenant on the farm, has not been found. Authorities have not confirmed whether the missing tenant, Jerome Farrand, is a suspect—"

"That's enough," Farrand said.

I didn't imagine it. It wasn't a blessed hallucination, it was real.

And I need help.

No, he thought. *I don't need help. We all need help.*

Father Murray muted the TV.

"What is it, Jerry? What does this . . . have to do with you."

Farrand looked at the younger priest, wondering what his reaction was going to be to this incredible . . . tale. "That's where I lived. What killed them . . . was coming for me."

"Oh, come on, you—"

Farrand looked up and he knew that his expression, the way his eyes narrowed into dark, resolute slits, silenced the other cleric.

"Listen," Farrand said. He spat the word out. Then, more gently. "Please, just . . . listen to me."

Father Murray sat down again.

Farrand shook his head and made a hollow laugh. "This may take some time. And Lord, I'm not sure we have a lot of time. But I need to tell you it all, as much as I know." He looked right into the priest's eyes. "Enough . . . so you understand. So you can help."

The priest nodded.

"Maybe you better get us some tea?" Farrand asked. "And some biscuits. I'm afraid I'm about to ruin your night's sleep."

"Yes." Father Murray picked up a black phone and called down to the housekeeper. Farrand waited.

When the priest finished talking to the cook, he turned to Farrand and said, "Okay."

"As I said, it will take some time. And then maybe you will help me." Farrand took a breath. "My involvement in this started not long after the war. It was nineteen forty-six. The world was still recovering. Nineteen forty-six, and I was a young priest, and I came . . . to Egypt . . . to the Valley of the Kings . . ."

And Father Murray sat there, and listened as the years melted away . . .

PART TWO

The Book of the Dead

NINE

October 1947
Valley of the Kings

Father Jerome Farrand, S.J., fell in love with Egypt from almost the first day he arrived. The post-war country simmered with the threat of other wars and hatreds, but the ancient world seemed larger than even the worldwide conflagration that had just ended.

There was no place in the world that he'd have rather been.

He had just been awarded his doctorate in archaeology from Georgetown, along with extensive work in ancient languages, and he was here because this expedition needed him. The fact that he was a priest meant nothing.

For Farrand, the excitement didn't end with the excavations. Even in modern times, the people of Egypt seemed to carry the feeling of a civilization millennia old. There was nothing he liked better than to wander through the twisting streets of Al Uqsur . . . Luxor—just soaking up the sounds and the smells.

Farrand knew that there were dangers ahead. Egypt had joined the struggle over what was then called Palestine.

And everyone who was familiar with the region knew that years of bloodshed and regional war lay ahead, despite the British attempt to create peace in the area.

You didn't have to be a fortune-teller to predict the wars, the pain, the suffering ahead.

Still, Farrand could lose himself in the wonderful work. The find that he was brought over to work on dated back to the late thirties. But as soon as the war broke out authorities with the Cairo Museum sealed the excavation. It was a subterranean, extensive tomb, perhaps a nobleman from the reign of Akhenaten. It was, everyone assumed, a find of modest importance that would have to wait until the world war ended and the desert once again became a battleground for only shifting sands and scorpions.

Or so they thought.

But as soon as the Egyptian-American-French team re-entered the chambers they discovered a number of oddities. One in particular disturbed the team. This was obviously not the burial chamber of some petty court nobleman. Not at all. They found, as expected, the odd pieces of furniture, the canopic jars, and the small treasure boxes. But then they discovered, recessed into the wall, other small chambers containing chests and jars.

The first jar contained the skull of a crocodilian, not really preserved but dried to a leathery toughness that would probably hold it together for a few more thousand years.

A second recessed chamber held a chest filled with what looked like small clawlike hands, at least a dozen of them. The archaeologists who examined that chest assumed they were the claws of some kind of monkey. Experts at the Museum of Natural History determined that the monkey was the now-extinct black moon monkey, a court favorite of the Egyptians.

And so it went, small recessed chambers filled with jars and chests containing parts of animals. They even uncovered a small silvery jewel box filled with scorpions' stingers.

Slowly the team realized that they were dealing with a

find of a different order, perhaps a find of real importance. They needed help.

Which is how Farrand found himself given this incredible opportunity. Farrand's specialty was ancient cults—not the major religious movements and revivals of the dynasties, but the small, splinter groups who worked behind the scenes, often to the detriment of the ruling powers.

Farrand was thrilled to join the team.

Except he was bothered by one thing, a thing that nagged at him.

He had seen the photos taken by the team, seen the sketches of the layout of the chamber. And he knew he had never seen anything like it. Not only that, there had never been a find at all like this, with its bazaarlike collection of animal parts. There was, he thought on the long flight over to England and then on to Cairo, something disturbing about all this.

But after weeks, his concerns receded. The work was exhilarating. Each day's careful exhumation brought new discoveries. The team moved slowly, taking care not to miss or destroy anything, little knowing that they were only meters away from a discovery that could change the world.

Weeks after his arrival, Farrand spent most days bent over shards of wall friezes, seeing things he had never seen before.

The first thing he noted in his long rambling letters back to his compatriots at Georgetown was that this material didn't seem to come from the reign of Akhenaten at all. Akhenaten was famous for three things: his beautiful queen, Nefertiti; the extended, almost deformed look to Akhenaten's head; and his risky endeavor to introduce monotheism to the Egyptian world. Some speculated that it was this move that led to his mysterious death, a regicide.

But a lot of what Farrand saw here seemed to come from another time completely, a period suffused with the idolatry of animals of all kinds. How else to explain the great archives of creatures that filled the chambers of this . . . well, what exactly was it?

That was the other mystery.

Whose chamber was this? It definitely didn't belong to a nobleman, or even a high courtier. There were none of the official documents that acknowledged that this was the tomb of some esteemed personage.

There was nothing to give a clue as to who, if anyone, might have been buried here. But Farrand knew that if they kept digging they would find something.

He just wasn't prepared for what they'd found.

It was a late evening, a balmy Egyptian evening just before the sun slips down below the hills of the Valley of the Kings, when the air turns cool. The work would stop within minutes. Farrand was piecing together a terracotta jigsaw puzzle, trying to fit twenty broken shards together, when there was a shout from within the chamber. Farrand knew that something exciting must have been found and hurried inside.

The last shafts of sunlight filled the entranceway. Farrand had to crouch down to make any progress into the inner chambers, to the interior walls now dotted with excavations. He saw a group huddled by one opening in the wall, shouting excitedly.

Farrand pushed close to the wall.

The Egyptian coleader of the excavation, Dr. Daloul, turned to Farrand with a giant grin.

"Do you see, Farrand . . . do you see what we have found!"

And actually he couldn't, not until he got down and looked into the small opening, leaving just enough room for the flashlight to send a diffuse stream of light inside.

And Farrand saw three tightly bound rolls. Papyri, a rare find, since most papyri get destroyed or eroded by time. A small chest was next to them. The artifacts looked perfect, protected by the wall of stone that surrounded them.

A young worker, more enthusiastic than trained, jabbered something at Daloul. "Azid wants to bring them out. Do you think . . ."

Farrand peered into the chamber. Either someone would have to reach in and grab the scrolls, or they'd have to excavate around them, risking the collapse of the small alcove.

Farrand stood up. "I don't know. Maybe we should try—"

But then Farrand heard a shriek, a horrifying scream. He turned to see Azid with his arm jammed into the opening. Something had happened. He began yelling, turning to the others with a horrified face.

"What is it?" Farrand said.

Daloul shrugged. "I don't know. He says something has grabbed him."

Daloul's answer was punctuated by another shriek from Azid who kept talking, pleading for help.

"He says . . . that it feels as if . . . something is eating him."

"Pull him out!"

But it was too late for that as Azid went flying back, ripping his hand free of the trap. His hand was still there, but now so mangled it was no longer recognizable as a hand. His screams filled the small chamber. The other workers pulled back . . . as if whatever was in that hole might slither out and come for them.

"Quick!" Daloul screamed. "Wrap his wound! Get him out now!"

The workers remained frozen for a moment and then one took a piece of cloth and wrapped Azid's hand. Then they picked up the sobbing, moaning man and carried him out to the entrance.

Farrand took the flashlight and leaned close to the opening.

"Father! Don't do that! There's something wrong here!"

"Yes, and I bet it's a trap. Some clever device to hurt anyone who tried to recover those scrolls. I want to see if I can spot the mechanism."

"Father Farrand, I'm afraid that what just happened . . . changes things."

Farrand turned to Daloul. "What do you mean?"

"I mean, that as the Egyptian authority here, I must see what happened to Azid and make sure that there are—"

Daloul looked around the cramped chamber "—no more 'traps,' as you say."

"What? You don't think this is booby-trapped?"

"I don't know, my friend. But for now . . . I want this site closed. Guarded. We will consider what to do. How best to . . . proceed."

Both men looked at the narrow hole in the stone. Farrand was sure that there was some clever mechanism inside, a small-scale version of the types of traps found in tombs like the pyramid of Cheops. They'd have to be careful, but there was nothing mysterious here.

But Daloul was immovable.

"Very well. But let me join the discussions."

Daloul nodded. "Certainly. But come out now. The sun is down. And I want this place . . . empty."

Daloul pointed the way for Farrand to leave while he and the workers followed.

The next day Farrand awakened to the noise of shouts and excited voices in the street. The hotel room had been stifling, suffocating, his sleep disturbed by the overwhelming heat.

He almost felt as if he had a hangover . . . there was a ringing in his ears. He had returned from the site early, but he felt awful now. He struggled to the window and pushed aside the sheer curtain.

The crowd talked wildly, gesturing at the Cairo paper one of them held.

Be a good time to know more than a smattering of Arabic.

But he did catch one word . . . "dead."

Someone in the town had been killed. But why was everyone so excited? If anything, post-war Egypt was a more dangerous place than before the war. Money was needed and some locals would do anything to get it.

Farrand pulled on a pair of trousers and walked out to the hallway.

A slight man in a fez—Ymir—walked by with a tray of tea.

"Good morning, Father," the server said.

"Morning," Farrand said.

Ymir smiled and started to move away.

"Excuse me . . . but what's all the excitement outside?"

The man's smile evaporated. "Oh, some local merchant was killed. People are upset."

Farrand nodded. "But this . . . upset?"

The man looked clearly discomfited. Farrand continued probing. "Anything unusual about it?"

The small man looked up and down the dark hallway as if checking if someone might be there, could hear him.

He made a small nervous smile. "There are legends, Father. Old legends that have lasted among my people for as long as people have been here." He took a step closer to Farrand. The priest looked at the pot of tea.

"Mind if I pour a cup?"

The man nodded. "These legends speak of a time long ago when man and animal were not in two different worlds. Those images you see on the tombs, on the great pyramids, the things you believe to be myth . . . Some of our people believe that it was all once true."

Farrand poured a small cup of the rich, deep brown tea. He dropped a chunk of sugar into it.

"People believe," Farrand asked, "that human and beast came together?"

The man nodded, and smiled again. "Crazy, no? But who knows where such beliefs come from." The priest could tell that maybe Ymir wasn't immune to such thoughts.

"So . . . what does this have to do with what's happening outside?"

Ymir looked around again then stepped closer to Farrand. "Last night, someone was killed. It happens, especially in the market quarter late at night. But it's how this person was killed."

Farrand sipped the tea.

"It was as if—and excuse me if I offend—as if the poor soul had been attacked by some creature. His limbs were torn away from his body in great tears. And then it looked like something pulled and chewed at his torso." Ymir took

93

a breath and the quiet hallways felt so close that Farrand had to take a deep breath.

"Couldn't it simply have been that he was attacked and some crazed killer took revenge on him for something, disfigured his body, and—"

But Ymir shook his head.

"No, Father. You see . . . when this poor soul was found, this man who no longer looked like a man was discovered, the authorities found something else. The man had used his finger . . . and his own blood to write a word on the stone."

Farrand licked his lips. He was beginning to understand why everyone in the streets was so upset.

"And what was that word?"

Ymir nodded. The end of his story had arrived. Farrand had asked a question, and he got his answer. And maybe he knew more than he wanted to.

"Father, the man had written the name . . . 'Horus'."

Horus, an ancient Egyptian animal deity. "Horus," Farrand repeated.

"Yes, Father. It was as if the poor soul wanted to say who did this . . . Horus, or one of his minions, one of the cruel gods of ancient times, returned once more."

Farrand looked at his teacup.

It was empty.

He had the feeling that somehow his life, his work in Egypt, had suddenly changed. In fact, he knew it had changed.

He just didn't know how much everything would change for him from that moment.

That same morning Farrand heard from Daloul incredible news.

The site had been looted, Daloul shrieked. Many things were taken.

Farrand asked about the scrolls.

"Those too! This is terrible."

"You should have let me try to remove them."

Daloul turned officious. "It's too late for that. This project has been ravaged." Then—a chilling moment—he looked at Farrand and said, "Your work here, good Father, is over."

Farrand nodded. With nothing left, the dig was finished. And after Daloul left, he sat in his room, growing even hotter with the warmth of the day, wondering what to do. Daloul was a fool to let such an incredible find get stolen, he thought.

But as soon as he had that realization, he knew it wasn't true.

The site hadn't been robbed. For a phenomenal sum of money, Daloul probably let someone remove the artifacts.

Farrand was convinced that that's what happened.

If he attempted to prove it, he'd join the poor travelers who fell victim to some "thief's" knife. And how would he gather evidence?

But he knew one thing. He couldn't leave Egypt. Not yet. Not when there were so many things that he didn't know.

The next day, there was another murder. This time, Ymir would not talk about the murder, turning hysterical when Farrand pressed him on details. But he gathered information from other sources . . . some embassy people talking at lunch, a tourist inquiring about checking out early.

A woman had been killed this time. The killing was different, though the details were sketchy. She was strangled by something thick. The ligature marks on her neck were as wide as a fire hose. But that's not what killed her. The young woman's head had been—incredibly—bitten off. Farrand also picked up another bit of information that chilled him more than anything in his adult life.

The man who was killed was an official with the Egyptian government in charge of dealing with all matters involving antiquities. The young woman was the Head Archivist at the Cairo Museum.

All of a sudden . . . the killings didn't seem random at all.

• • •

That same night, at dinner Farrand made notes on his fears and suspicions, growing stronger daily.

On his way back, he got lost.

Getting lost in the backstreets was not that hard. But Farrand had been here for months. He knew his way around.

And yet—here he was, wandering around narrow, twisting alleyways, with no moon in the sky. After a few minutes, he stopped.

Got to get my bearings, he thought.

So preoccupied, he thought, *I must have taken a wrong turn somewhere.*

He looked around for something to guide him, but each twisting maze-path looked the same. He took a step.

And he *heard* a step. Not far behind him. He took another.

And now he heard the sound of feet. But not the sound of shoe or sandal on stone. But something softer, something padded, followed by a scratch.

His heart started racing. It was so dark here.

His mental images of the two slain people came to mind.

Of course, he thought.

Somehow it made sense to him . . . that he had to be killed.

Then other things came to mind. The descriptions of the bodies, the brutal, animal nature of the killings.

It gave him an ice-cold blast of adrenaline.

He started running. It didn't matter which direction, they all looked the same.

Farrand immediately heard the sound of those feet behind, clearly racing, clearly animal—and then something new, the sound of something breathing hard, panting.

Farrand prayed. For a light, for people.

He came to another junction, still dark, the curved passageways stretching deeper into darkness. He couldn't stop, simply taking one and running, whispering prayers to God as though he were some simple-minded religious peasant.

The footfalls were closer, just behind him. He almost imagined he could feel breathing.

Another junction, and he cut sharply right without a clue where it led.

But he saw a glimmer of light, then heard voices. He bolted as fast as he could, stumbling into a lit street with a café, people outside, drinking, smoking, looking at Farrand—a crazed man.

He ran to a café table and fell into a seat, turning to look at the thing, this beast that had to be behind him.

But nothing came.

A waiter appeared and asked in Arabic, then English, "Want a drink?"

Farrand nodded. "Yes," he said. He kept watching the alleyway . . . but nothing emerged into the light.

And then, on his last days in Egypt, Farrand's life—what would be his life—changed forever.

The killings continued, only now Farrand had the sick realization that he knew what was going on, knew that it had something to do with the scrolls found in the tomb.

Farrand avoided the streets at night. His attempts to reach Daloul, to learn what was happening, went unanswered. The Cairo government did its best to cover up the murders, but already the foreign press was printing stories about the strange Egyptian killings.

And Farrand realized this: *If I don't get out of here, I'm dead.*

Whatever was happening here he couldn't deal with alone. He even tried sending a telegram back to New York—but Ymir returned with it, an odd expression on his face, explaining that the message couldn't be sent now . . . that there were problems.

Farrand resolved the next day to leave. He couldn't deal with what was going on here by himself.

That last night, Farrand got a call. At first he didn't recognize the muffled voice, and then he knew it was Daloul, struggling to breathe. He asked Farrand to meet him, that he must meet him. Now. Or it would be too late.

Right, thought Farrand, As if it made any sense going

out in the night. He told Daloul that he wouldn't come to him.

"You must! If you value that . . . God of yours, you will come to me. I am dying, Farrand. But I must tell you what happened . . . what's happening . . ." The man started coughing.

Farrand thought a moment. He could plan a path that took him past the brightly lit cafés and the shops that stayed open late in the old quarter. There would be only a small narrow stretch where it would be . . . secluded.

"Okay, Daloul. I'll be there."

"Good," the man said, and coughed again.

The line went dead, and Farrand hurried out into the night.

The wind blowing through the ancient streets was cool, a chilly desert breeze that made its serpentine way through the streets, nearly a living thing.

Men in the cafés looked up at Farrand as he hurried by. Why so fast, they must be wondering? So late at night, where could you be hurrying to?

Farrand didn't slow his pace as he moved into a part of the old quarter dotted with tiny shops that seemed perpetually open. Ahead he'd have to turn down a small alleyway to meet Daloul.

All of a sudden, there were no lights, no people.

Farrand thought of stopping. *This is too dangerous,* he thought. And then another thought: *This is a trap.*

But then, at the next curve in the alleyway, he saw a figure standing in a doorway.

Farrand stopped.

"Daloul?"

"Come . . . closer . . ." Daloul croaked.

Farrand took a few cautious steps closer. He could barely make out that it was in fact Daloul, it was so dark.

"Maybe we should go back a bit, to the cafés," Farrand suggested.

"No . . ." Daloul said, his voice clogged, guttural. "We must talk here." Farrand was about to protest when he saw something glinting in the darkness, something shiny at the man's midsection. He was bleeding—no, it was worse than that—he looked as if he had to hold himself together.

"Daloul, my God, we must get you some help."

But Daloul shook his head. "No, Father. It is too late for me. Way too late."

"No, we can—"

Daloul reached out and grabbed Farrand's wrist, surprising him with his strength.

"Listen, I don't have a lot . . ." he coughed ". . . of time. You must *listen*."

"Go on, Daloul. Tell me."

"I let those scrolls be stolen. Do you know their value— do you have any idea of what they were worth?"

"I do."

"But you were wrong." Daloul made a sick laugh. "We both were wrong."

"What do you mean?"

A sound echoed from down the alleyway, a window being shuttered against the cold. Farrand shivered.

"Please, Daloul—let me take you to a hospital, some—"

"No. You must listen. There isn't any time. Those scrolls weren't just any ancient texts . . . they were the missing books."

"The missing books?"

Daloul coughed. "From the Book of the Dead. The cursed pages dealing with the alchemy, the merging of man and animal, the creation of the new gods . . ."

Farrand shook his head. The Egyptian Books of the Dead were always known to be incomplete. But many scholars felt that the so-called missing books were apocryphal. Some scholars thought that they never existed. But if they did, the references in the main texts referred to a gift from the dark gods, a way to give man powers through merging with animals. Egyptian ruins were littered with carvings of jackal-headed humans, and eagles with arms, and other animal-human combinations, all part of the bizarre cult religions of Ancient Egypt.

Myth, like so many ancient legends.

"Those scrolls," Daloul said. "They were the lost books. And as soon as we removed them, people came to us and showed us their power."

Farrand thought of the other night, and the bizarre murders. He felt completely unprepared for dealing with Daloul's hushed words.

"The killings . . . are they part of this?"

Daloul nodded. "Those pages could create these . . . things!" His voice rose to a terrible shriek. "I saw it myself. It was powerful, amazing, a wonder! But those who might figure out what was happening had to die. You—" Daloul looked right at Farrand "—You were next."

Farrand licked his lips. *I should be dead,* he thought. *I should be as dead as any of the others.*

"B-but something protected you. For now. Your faith, something holy . . . I don't know. But as they grow stronger, they will rip you to pieces like all the others."

"Why, Daloul? Where are they? I must get help, stop them . . ."

Did this mean that Farrand believed the man? Was all this true? Or was Farrand becoming as crazed as all the other superstitious Egyptians? Crouched close to Daloul, he didn't know.

"No. You can't. They are too strong here for you alone. And besides . . . it's too late . . ."

Another sound from the alleyway. Farrand took a breath.

"Too late? What do you—"

"Tonight, they are moving the scrolls, the powerful scrolls. Tonight they have left on a ship. They will go to a place of power, a place where their demon-infested kind can take over, rule, crush . . . Humanity will be no more."

"Moving? Tonight?"

"Yes. The ship has already set sail. But I did something . . . that they don't know about. You can follow the ship, track it. The scrolls must not ever reach your world!"

"The ship, Daloul. What is the name of the ship?"

Did he really believe this, Farrand thought? Or was he simply humoring the dying man?

Daloul reached out his hidden arm as if to support himself.

Except the arm wasn't an arm. Farrand stepped back. He saw the light reflect off the dull-greenish . . . hide. Daloul's arm seemed to be something from a lizard. Where there should have been a hand, Farrand saw three claws that opened and closed slowly, almost begging to hold on to something.

"Please, Farrand. Let me hold on . . ."

Farrand watched in disbelief as the claws closed around his wrist and Daloul took a step closer to the priest.

"The name of the ship is . . . the *Maroc*. I don't know where it is bound. It must not—"

Daloul groaned.

"Must not arrive."

And then Daloul slid to the floor, his lizard hand still clutching, nearly pulling Farrand down.

Farrand stood there in the darkness. He waited a moment, and then Daloul was dead.

The strong smell of blood filled the alleyway.

The *Maroc*, he thought. Was there any doubt that this horror was true? Not anymore. And worse, Farrand knew that he was maybe the only one who could somehow stop it.

He turned around and started running back the way he came, back past the cafés filled with men talking, drinking, smoking, unaware of the horror so close by.

TEN

For a long time Father Murray stood by the window in the reception room, so very quiet.

Looking out the window. Below, people were still streaming from the London pubs, searching for cabs, hunting for a late night meal. A light rain spattered the window.

Finally, he turned to Farrand.

He smiled. "You know, I had heard stories about you and your obsession."

Farrand didn't smile back. "Oh, is that what they called it?"

"Some did. I'm afraid your pursuit of those artifacts and the ship became something of a joke, at least when I was at Georgetown. Though none of us heard what you have told me tonight. These fantastic details . . . that's new."

"I'm glad that I became something to amuse the priests who came after me."

Father Murray walked back to Farrand and sat down on the intricately brocaded couch. "No, Farrand. There was more to it than that. There was also this great sense of loss, a brilliant archaeologist . . . lost."

"I wasn't the one who was lost. The Church was blind."

The priest nodded. "So why do you come to me now, Farrand? What do you think the Jesuits, or the Church, can do for you now?"

Farrand looked directly at the younger priest. And he described what happened the night before. "They came to kill me . . . preparing the way. They had to search long and hard to find me, but when it was important enough, they did. With me dead, the last link to that discovery—to what was going to happen—would be removed."

Father Murray took a breath. "And what is going to happen?"

Farrand didn't answer right away. Outside, the faint rain had sputtered to a stop, leaving only tiny drops on the window, shrinking. The sky had the slightest touch of light. A long night was about to melt into gray morning.

Farrand spoke quietly, knowing the importance of not overdramatizing, of not losing this potential ally.

"I don't know what is in the scrolls. I just know that, in those first days, some sick force capable of merging human and beast reentered the earth."

"A force?"

Farrand nodded. "I know. It's not fashionable to believe in the . . . power of evil, in its raw existence—"

"Don't count me among those."

Farrand made a shallow laugh. "I thought the modern Church didn't believe in such things."

"Evil will always be with us. Go on about this force . . ."

"About something I don't know much about? I've spent decades researching . . . and I know so little. But I know this, Father. If that ship has been found, if those scrolls have survived . . ."

"What, Farrand? What do you think will happen?"

Now the old priest got up. It was a struggle to push himself up and walk to the window. Morning light now illuminated the dozens of tiny drops still clinging to the window.

"What will happen? I've often asked myself that. I only

knew about the horrible vision contained in the Books of the Dead, the half that we possess . . ."

"The vision?"

Farrand nodded. He felt so tired, so defeated. He wondered if maybe it was already too late.

"A vision of hell. On earth. The struggle between good and evil over . . . forever. Evil triumphant."

And with that, the old man coughed. He looked at Father Murray, coughed again. A sharp pain bloomed in his chest.

Another cough and the old man collapsed to the floor.

The sound of the bell woke Derek up. He looked at the digital clock. Midnight. He had been asleep for only an hour. He grabbed a remote and clicked on the monitor across the room.

He saw Nick, standing outside Legacy House.

Derek got out of bed and hurried downstairs to the front door. The bell kept sounding, eerie in the stillness of the mansion so late at night.

He opened the door to see Nick looking scared.

"What is it? Come in."

Nick entered the building. His eyes were wide and Derek couldn't ever recall seeing Nick looking really frightened. Now he looked terrified. Derek shut the door behind him.

"Something happened?"

Nick nodded. "In my apartment." He looked at Derek and shook his head. "Don't laugh, but what do you know about rats, Derek?"

"Rats? They're rodents, they gnaw, they eat almost everything."

"Right. All that, and they have a nest, and they slowly will work themselves to sources of food and water. That I know. When I was on kitchen duty during basic training . . . in Virginia. We had a big rat problem." He took a breath. "My apartment was just overrun with rats."

"What?"

"They were everywhere, like a swarm of insects. I thought I'd go mad."

"Could it have been—"

"A hallucination? No. Not possible. They were real. The bodies of the ones I killed are still around the apartment. No, Derek. They were real. The attack was real. Just like the shark attack."

"Come into the Communications Center."

He walked through the holographic door with Nick following.

"This isn't a coincidence," Derek said. "Philip's incidents, your attacks, something is moving against us. But why?"

"What has Rachel found out?"

"Nothing really. Not yet, anyway."

"Let me go East and work with her."

"Nick, we have no evidence that these things are linked."

"No. Except my intuition . . . and yours. Let me go. I could help her. And she might be in danger."

Derek sat down at the long conference table.

"Right. She might use help and she might be in danger—but I don't want you going out there, or Philip—not till we know more."

"But I was attacked, damn it!"

"Precisely. Something is interested in you. Until we know the reason, you stay here."

"Then who will you send?"

"Alex." Derek smiled. "God knows she needs some time away from her terminal." He looked at Nick. "And that means you can man the network."

"If you insist."

"And stay here while Alex is gone. Just don't break anything!"

And finally Nick smiled.

Callie Peterson woke up. Her bed felt clammy and cool though she had a huge Bavarian down comforter covering her. She lay there for a moment. What woke her up, she wondered. She always slept so soundly, right through the night.

What made her stir tonight?

She looked at the clock. Four A.M. What a dismal, horrible time. It was around this time that she lost her husband. She had sat with him all night as the cancer finally claimed him. He squeezed her hand, she woke up and he was looking right at her. His lips were always so cracked, so terribly and hopelessly dry.

But that night he smiled.

She knew what it was.

Good-bye.

He squeezed one more time, and then shut his eyes. The death rattle came suddenly, a real spasm. With his hand locked on hers, it was as if he wanted to hold on to her.

Then it was over. He was gone. And it was 4:03 A.M.

Am I dying, she wondered. *Is this my . . . wake-up call to die?*

But no. She felt fine. Every day was a gift. And she savored each one.

She looked around the dark bedroom. Was it a noise, some critter outside?

She sat up. She saw the computer screen blinking. She left it on as usual, connected to her T1 line, picking up various things she used for her work. But the sound was off. If new images came, there would have been no tone, nothing to wake her.

Four A.M. What Ingmar Bergman dubbed . . . the hour of the wolf. The darkest hour before dawn.

She slid out of her bed, sliding her feet into her slippers and walked over to her terminal and sat down.

As long as I'm up, she thought, *let's see what's come in.*

She wriggled her toes in the slippers. *So darn chilly,* she thought. She moved her mouse and the screen came to life showing her EudoraPro program. She saw lots of mail since she went to bed, more satellite stills, some sonographic soundings from the Aleutians where the U.S. Navy had been doing some earthquake studies.

In preview mode, she saw a request for more information about the location of that wreck that popped up in the last satellite scan.

She opened the mail.

It wasn't from the Navy, or NOAA, or any of her usual

customers. No, this was from someone she didn't know. And she didn't recognize the URL of the agency, *www.dataarchive.org*.

They wanted the coordinates, the scan, her interpretation. She started writing back to them.

Sorry. But I have to process the data to create a floor map image. Then, if you send your request through—

She stopped.

What was the expression? She forgot so many things these days.

Then it came to her . . .

. . . the usual channels.

She sent the mail.

Why the interest in this old wreck? she wondered. She opened up her folder with the recent scans.

First she opened a recent scan showing the precipitous slope of one part of the Bermuda Rise. Then another. She was the first to take the Navy readings and turn them into a map of sea floor. That map became the worldwide standard. Now she knew that it was littered with errors. All these new detailed findings would change that.

She flipped to the next thumbnail.

There it was . . . the object. A ship. *What ship?* she wondered.

Was there any way she could find out? Of course there was. It was late, she was up—and she didn't have anything really to do.

And as Callie went on the Web, the hour of the wolf turned into the fiery orange of dawn.

ELEVEN

Rachel tried to duck her panel the next day, but the leader made her feel so guilty that she went and added her thoughts on the ancient debate of talk therapy versus pharmaceuticals. When it grew heated, she tuned out.

And she was surprised to find that she was thinking about not just Martina Popov, but also her brother. She wished they could have gone to the gallery early, but the panel—and the obligatory coffee and questions after—tied up a good chunk of the day.

When she got back there were two messages on the hotel voice mail.

The first was from Derek saying that Alex was getting an early flight out to help her.

Help? she wondered.

Does Derek have that little confidence in me that he has to send Alex out to help? I can't talk to some people and get some information without someone holding my hand?

She called Derek back on his personal line and left a message.

"Derek, I'm doing fine here, there's no reason for Alex

to fly out. I even—" she wondered whether she should tell them about Greg. No, she decided, it might confuse things. "I think it's a wasted trip. Probably a dead end here. Call me."

God, probably too late to stop Alex from taking an unnecessary trip. *Nice confidence they have in me,* she thought.

She went back to her message box and listened to message number two.

It was Greg explaining that he was going to be stuck at a late conference that he couldn't dodge. They could go to the gallery tomorrow—or if she went alone he could meet her back at the hotel.

She didn't want to wait.

She called Greg's number and got his voice mail. She listened to the obligatory, "I'm either away from my desk or on another call—"

"Hi, Greg—sorry you can't come." She took a breath. "I'd like you to be with me." Did she really mean to send him a message? Did she sound so terribly desperate? "I'm going to go talk to them tonight. But come by the hotel. We'll have a drink and I'll tell you what I learned. If anything. Bye."

There, she thought. *Hope I don't sound too much like I want to see him again.*

She took out her subway map and plotted her path down to SoHo.

Derek stood by the gate and touched Alex's shoulder.

Alex smiled. "Do I mind going? Not at all. You usually stick me behind a terminal. And besides, I love New York. Heard from Rachel?"

He debated telling her that Rachel wasn't exactly excited that she was coming.

"I left her a message—and she sent a message back. So she knows."

Alex nodded, and Derek saw in her eyes that he wasn't fooling her.

The loudspeaker announced final boarding.

"I have you in first class."

"Only the best, and besides that way I can do some work. I'm gathering all this bizarre information on animal symbols. Might be useful—once we know what we're dealing with."

Derek looked at the gate. No one else boarding.

"You better go. I'll keep my cell phone by me, and on, all the time. Give me a call tonight as soon as you hook up with Rachel."

"Will do—"

Then Derek gave her a quick hug and—after a quick hug back—Alex dashed to the gate and vanished.

He waited there for a few minutes . . . not simply thinking about Alex, but also about all this.

Something about this felt wrong. Things happen to Nick and Philip, Rachel starts investigating, Alex goes to help her—it all seemed as though forces were moving the Legacy into and out of position.

And if that was true . . . the big question was:

What are those forces?

And that Derek knew nothing about.

He turned away from the now deserted gate, troubled, perplexed, and even a bit scared.

The number 6 local train wasn't running. At least that's what Rachel thought that she heard the loudspeaker squawking with some scratchy sounds that were barely intelligible.

She dug out her map.

The number 6 wasn't running. Which meant that she'd have to . . . what? Take an express?

And then what?

She looked for an express stop that would put her within walking distance of SoHo. Was the Brooklyn Bridge the closest? *Maybe I'll buy it while I'm there.*

"Scuse me . . . miz . . ."

She turned to see a man all curved and hunched over. His filthy black overcoat was only matched by his out of control and unkempt beard. Rachel looked around. The platform was filled with lots of respectable people, businessmen, and young mothers, couples—why did this guy target me?

She turned away. That's what you were supposed to do.

"Scuse me, miz . . ." he said louder.

Rachel took a step away. Then another. One more "scuse me" and she'd start screaming at the bum.

But then—

He spoke again. But now his voice was no longer a guttural, raspy, whiskey-ravaged thing. Now it was a gentle, soothing voice.

"You look lost."

She turned to the voice expecting to see the bum replaced by some well-heeled businessman.

But no—the bum was still there. Looking right up at her with rheumy red-veined eyes.

"Are you—" that voice again "—lost?"

It was a voice that she had to respond to.

"No. I'm not. I mean, I'm trying to get to—"

"Don't get lost," the voice suggested. "You don't want to get lost here."

Rachel nodded. "No, I don't." She backed away. But the voice continued. "Because if you get lost, no one will ever, ever find you."

Her heart raced. Her skin felt cold, clammy. She thought she might faint.

She remembered the words that the image of Martina said to Philip. "I am not lost . . ."

The bum took a lurching step closer to her.

"Gotz . . . sum change?"

The voice was transformed again, back to generic alky-bum. An express train screamed into the station and, as soon as the doors slid open, Rachel hurried inside.

Rachel ended up traveling down to the Brooklyn Bridge, eating up more time, taking just a moment to appreciate the bridge, before getting a cab to travel back uptown to SoHo.

When the cab crossed Canal Street all the blocks were locked in traffic hell. The only thing that seemed to be moving were the hands of the drivers pressing on their horns.

"I'll get out here and walk," Rachel said. She dug out some money while the recorded voice of Judd Hirsch reminded her to check for her valuables.

She was out before his cheery memo was done.

She walked briskly up Broadway, past the collection of cheapo export shops stocking everything from Furby knockoffs and no-name Walkmans to silk scarves and bins of masking tape. But after a block, Broadway morphed into a more genteel, hip place. She passed a French bistro that was actually a teaching restaurant, and then tiny clothing stores selling little nothing dresses for the tiniest of bodies.

You'd have to be twelve to shop here, she thought. *Or have the body of a twelve-year-old.*

By the time she got to Spring Street, hipness was in full flower, with the dominant clothing color ultra-cool black. It was past five P.M., and the sidewalks were almost impassable with the young and those who wished they still were.

She turned left on Spring. The Okthoro Gallery was near the corner of Wooster, occupying the biggest building on the street.

As she got close, she looked up at the building. It looked like one of those giant loft/warehouses, yet the gallery took up little space, only the ground floor.

So what was upstairs?

Other treasures? A private disco?

She got to the door of the gallery. A small sign announced PRIVATE SHOWING IN PROGRESS—BY INVITATION ONLY.

Damn, she thought. She watched a tall man and an even taller woman, both reed thin and dressed in pants that seemed glued to their legs, walk in, handing the guard at the door a white card.

As Rachel stood there, frozen by her indecision, she wondered if maybe Derek was right.

I can't cut it by myself. No initiative.

Okay, she thought, *if initiative is what it takes then that's what I'll have to get—from somewhere.*

She walked up to the door and opened it.

Farrand opened his eyes. He looked around the room. Was this a hospital? The walls were bare except for a simple cross. He moved his right arm and noticed the attached IV drip. He craned his head around and saw the clear bag of sugar water, half full.

What happened to me? he thought. *I was talking to Tom Murray—and, right . . . I collapsed. And now I'm in a hospital, or maybe still in the Jesuit building.* He hoped that it was the latter since the hospital might be harder to get out of.

And get out he must.

If Murray wasn't going to help him, he had to get out soon.

Farrand felt around for some kind of buzzer, something to call for a help. No buzzer. Good. Probably not a hospital. Then getting out wouldn't be that hard. He'd call for help—but not right away.

It had been stupid to come here.

He was alone.

Alone, and—God—so old. He'd have to do something about this by himself.

He should pray. But first, he had to plan . . .

In the expansive first class of the 747 plane, Alex refused the "welcome aboard" champagne, the wine with dinner, and barely touched what looked like a halfway decent cordon bleu.

Instead, she used the space to spread out all the printouts she had brought with her, trying to make some sense of what had been happening.

She knew that Derek was worried.

Derek had seen . . . everything. He didn't worry easy.

Most of the pages showed illustrations from the early Egyptian dynasties, before the brief revolution of Akhenaten. Amidst the stylized drawings of pharaohs and courtiers, she saw the classic illustrations of the half-human, half-animal creatures of Egyptian myth.

The strange myths and religions of Ancient Egypt. Pretty incredible stuff.

But was there any evidence that it wasn't all myth?

Not really. You could search all of Egyptian history and find nothing pointing to any secret metaphysical experiments, nothing that recalled the experiments of the Island of Dr. Moreau.

Nothing, that is, save the rumored contents from the missing parts of Ancient Egyptian texts.

Still, the more Alex studied the reproductions of friezes and artifacts from Egyptian tombs, the more she was struck by something odd.

The animal-human figures were supposed to be gods.

And yet . . . they're shown interacting on a daily basis with the human rulers—and, in some scenes, acting almost as if they were counseling the rulers. The pose was almost . . . naturalistic. It wasn't the way you'd portray a mythological god.

She opened up her slim Sony notebook computer. She loved this new toy, nearly thin as a pad of yellow paper. It was her favorite traveling companion. She had already scoured the Web for background about what were called "the underworld gods." These animalistic deities, some with goat heads, others with the talons of an eagle, were—according to most scholars—thought to protect the king.

But there were a few dissenting scholars.

One Oxford scholar, Dr. Edward Weeks, thought that gods like Thoth and Anubis didn't protect the king as much as control him. And the reason for the great tombs was that the priests of the gods convinced the pharaohs that they would live forever.

That deal was in exchange for something. Or so Weeks suggested.

Alex opened another folder in her Word files, packed with a rambling collection of mystical animal references she had gathered from the Net. She scrolled through images from the Aztec and Mayan cultures, more images of human-animal deities, and more propaganda about an afterlife ruled by these gods. She found similar religious beliefs in Celtic and even African society.

What did it all mean . . . if anything?

If Nick's animal attacks had a message, could they connect to this mythology?

Or was it something else? Was this trail a dead end? A lot would depend on what Rachel was finding out.

"Excuse me . . ."

Alex turned to the man sitting across the aisle. The first-class seat next to her was empty, which was great for work and she certainly didn't feel like talking.

"I couldn't help but notice all that ancient art you were looking at."

Alex nodded. "Yes, I—" She didn't know what to say. Except, maybe, go away . . .

"Are you a historian?"

I wish, thought Alex. *It would certainly make looking at all this ancient art less disturbing.*

"No. I'm just working on a project—"

The man smiled. A businessman, making chit-chat, maybe hoping for something more?

She could tell he was about to ask if he could sit next to her.

"And I've got a lot of work to do."

The man made a big O with his mouth. "Then I won't bother you."

Alex smiled. *Thanks for taking the hint.*

She turned back to her notebook computer.

Now, back to the rats and sharks. Do they have any special metaphysical significance?

She turned her search program loose on the jumble of documents.

The security guard smiled at Rachel. "Invitation, please?"

Rachel smiled back. She had considered lying. I lost it. Yup, the invitation just blew away somewhere in those nasty train tunnels. But she needed to speak to Martina's boss.

"No, I'm not here for the—" she looked around. A small group of people stood in the gallery, gathered in small groups chatting. If it was an opening, it looked mighty small. "I need to talk to the director."

"Oh," the guard said, not losing a bit of his smile, "I'm afraid Dr. Whitney won't be able to see anyone tonight, certainly not without an appointment."

Rachel noticed the small clusters of people taking notice of her entrance. She also checked the artifacts on display. If originals—and not reproductions—they were incredible. In the center of the room a giant ram-headed deity sat atop a squat throne while assorted friezes hung on the wall.

Rachel turned back to the guard. "No, you don't understand. I'm here for the—" and here she raised her voice "—the Popov family? Martina Popov?"

The guard's face fell.

"Still, you must make—"

Rachel shook her head. Funny, after you've faced demons a burly security guard wasn't so fierce at all.

"No. I want to talk with Dr. Whitney. Just for a few minutes and then—"

"Paul, what is it?"

Rachel turned in the direction of the voice. She watched a woman in a crisp business suit walk toward her. The woman wasn't young but still she looked striking, New York sleek, with perfect blonde hair, cut short, and—as she got closer—piercing jet-black eyes.

"Yes, can I help you?"

Rachel was aware of the people standing so quietly now in the room. She took a breath. "Yes, I think you can. I'm helping the Popovs and—"

Dr. Whitney took Rachel's arm. Rachel felt the strong, assured grip as the woman guided her off to the side. She saw one of the guests, a young woman maybe still in her teens, look over, a concerned expression on her face. For a moment, Rachel's eyes locked on the young woman. She turned away.

"Look, I don't know who you are, but—"

"Dr. Rachel Corrigan."

"Doctor?"

"Psychiatrist."

"Very nice. But I'm having a small, private showing and your timing couldn't be worse."

Rachel looked around again. She wished Greg was here to help.

"I'm sorry that I'm interfering with your show. But Martina Popov—your assistant—disappeared, and every day that goes by without finding her is a day lost. And that, as I'm sure you'll agree, is a hell of a lot more important than your show."

Rachel didn't realize that she was building to such a heated climax. But she took an instant dislike to this woman.

"Are you with the police?"

"No. I'm just a friend of the family." She was getting good at lying. "And I know you'd like to help the family."

Dr. Whitney nodded. "Okay then. Let me . . . greet everyone here, and then we can go back to my office and talk. Agreed?"

"Sounds great. By the way, is all this stuff original?"

"Yes. And it's all legal, too. Dating back to the great finds of the nineteenth century."

"Glad to hear that . . ."

And Rachel strolled the exhibit while waiting for Dr. Whitney to get free.

"Would you like a cordial?" the flight attendant asked. Alex looked up from her laptop screen.

"No, thanks." Though she would love one. A bit of brandy, a few hours snoozing in the big seat. But she had so much more she wanted to look at before arriving at Kennedy. She wanted to fire off a report to Derek as soon as she landed. If Philip and Nick were in some kind of danger, the more they knew the better.

She looked at her screen again.

She started cycling through the collection of downloaded images. There didn't seem to be any connection between the Mayan or Aztec images, other than both cultures had some kind of animal worship and imagery showing animal-like deities.

She thought of Thor Heyerdahl's experiment . . . he set sail in a replica of an ancient ship attempting to travel from Egypt to the Western Hemisphere in an effort to determine if precursors of Ancient Egyptians could have journeyed to Central and South America, bringing art, culture, their calendar, their religion.

She flipped to another image.

The picture showed a charming deity called "the devourer of the dead." Alex stared at it, it was so disturbing. A prone human body topped with this elongated snout. Creepy, even here, five miles up.

The plane jiggled a bit. A little ripple.

"Whoops, lost some of my martini," the businessman across the aisle said.

Another jiggle and the seat-belt light came on.

Alex already had her belt on. Always did during a flight . . . ever since she heard that story about the plane on its way to Hawaii that lost its top, the ceiling just *ripped* off, sending all the unbuckled people flying away.

Now a bigger bump.

The first-class flight attendant walked down the aisle checking that seat belts were in fact on. She stopped by the businessman.

"Sir, would you put your seat belt on?"

"Oh, I've hit worse on the Long Island Sound. Say, can I get a re—"

The captain came on the intercom.

"Folks, we seem to have run into a patch of turbulence—"

The plane hit another bump, and this time the cabin tilted to the left. Alex locked her hands on her computer. The bounce made the pilot stop.

"Er, and we're going to try to climb a bit to see if we can get out—"

Another bump. Another pause.

"Out of it. But we'd like to ask that you keep your seat belts fastened until we turn the light off."

Alex felt the plane tilt slightly, beginning its climb.

Okay, she thought. *The plane's climbing—but how far can it go? How much higher can it fly?*

But as it climbed things seemed to smooth out. No more bumps. *Maybe we just needed a few hundred feet,* Alex thought. *Let me get back to my work and—*

Then—it was like the plane smashed into an oncoming wave.

A loud thud, the plane tilted back, then Alex felt the sickening sensation as the plane dropped. She gripped the notebook tight. The man across the aisle groaned.

Little pinging noises filled the cabin, everyone clamoring for the flight attendant, some help, some reassurance.

Alex saw the attendant—a grim look on her face—struggling down the aisle.

I hate this, Alex thought. *Hate. It.*

The plane rocked right at an angle that Alex had never experienced in any flight. Maybe in an amusement park—but not in a goddamned plane.

She looked across the aisle.

The businessman was trying to get his belt buckled. Struggling to find one end buried in his seat. The attendant was halfway to him, supporting herself by wedging her arms against the overhead luggage bins.

Which was when the plane did a nosedive, a sick rollercoaster dip that had the seat belt digging into Alex's gut.

The man across the aisle flew out of his seat.

He smacked his head into the overhead bins and then tumbled over the seat in front of him.

Everyone was screaming now, crying.

Alex allowed the thought to . . . exist.

I'm going to die. Somewhere over the frozen, jagged peaks of the Rockies . . . I'm going to die.

The flight attendant, her arm wedge failed, had been thrown against the cockpit.

No comforting words from the pilot.

Now the plane did just the reverse maneuver, rearing back, nose up, as if . . . *we better get some altitude or we'll all be eating rock.*

Alex felt something wet on her cheek.

Down to her lip.

She tasted it. Salty.

I'm crying, God, I'm crying—because—I'm going to to die.

The businessman flew back now, landing in his seat upside down. Alex looked over quickly and saw blood around his neck. God . . . was he dead?

But she quickly looked forward, as if thinking that might somehow have something to do with how the plane would fly.

It steadied.

Still climbing. Getting away from those mountains, only feet away from those peaks . . .

She couldn't look out the window.

Wouldn't ever dare to do that.

Not to see how close they were.

Still climbing.

The pilot came on.

"Folks, please—"

Two words.

A tease.

As the plane flipped left.

The movement caught Alex by surprise and she felt her laptop go flying, smashing into the window before landing on the empty seat beside her.

The plane was tilted left . . . feeling like 40 . . . maybe 45 degrees.

The plane was filled with crying, hysterical people.

A bump adding to the fun of the bank.

Alex looked down to her computer notebook.

She saw the last image she had been looking at.

The devourer of the dead. Then—the image faded.

So slowly.

While Alex watched.

As it changed . . .

TWELVE

Rachel entered Dr. Whitney's office in the back of the gallery.

She had expected an elegant room decorated in modern furniture suitable for seducing money from fat-cat collectors.

Instead it looked like something out of Indiana Jones. Her desk was piled high with books, clay artifacts, and shards from friezes. The woman's desk chair was a simple wooden chair. A similar chair faced Dr. Whitney's desk.

"Go on, Dr. Corrigan, sit . . ."

Rachel took the other chair.

"Now, let me be very clear. As far as I can tell, you are not with the police. The police are, I believe, the ones investigating this matter. So I'm not too sure what responsibility—if any—I have to tell you anything."

The woman was powerful, used to getting exactly what she wanted, Rachel thought.

"I know. I appreciate you seeing me. I'm trying to help the Popovs. They are very worried."

Dr. Whitney took out a pack of cigarettes. She opened the box and took out one.

She didn't offer one to Rachel . . . and didn't ask her if she minded if she smoked.

I don't like this bitch, Rachel thought.

The woman blew the bluish smoke into the air.

"They should be worried. Martina was—is—a very disturbed girl. She lived a life of fantasy, craving excitement. I can't tell you how many mornings she staggered in here after partying until nearly dawn, sleeping with who knows what. I tried to talk to her. But—there was no talking to Martina."

"You told her parents this?"

The woman smiled condescendingly. "One doesn't tell bad stories about someone's little girl, Dr. Corrigan. I'd think you, of all people, would know that."

"Only if the stories are true."

Dr. Whitney took a long, slow drag. She smiled at Rachel.

"Trust me. They were true."

"So what happened to her?"

Dr. Whitney looked away. "With Martina, anything was possible. You play in the woods, in the wild . . . and you might get lost."

Rachel froze.

She remembered what Philip said . . . the words that vision of Martina said, so clearly, an appeal for help.

Maybe a warning.

I am not lost.

"Lost?"

Dr. Whitney smiled an ice queen smile. *What a bitch,* thought Rachel. *And there's more to their relationship than employee and boss. But what?*

"On any night, a dozen bad things could have happened to Martina. When you crave excitement, sometimes you find it." Puff. "Too much of it."

"Then, where would I—"

Dr. Whitney stood up.

"If you'll excuse me, I have to get back to our opening."

She walked to the door, opened it, and held it there, waiting for Rachel.

There was more here, Rachel knew—a lot more. But it was doubtful she'd learn it now.

"Can I talk to you again?"

"Doubtful," Dr. Whitney said. She smiled. "Only if the police say I must . . ."

Rachel walked out the door.

And walking out to the gallery she noticed . . . felt something.

Everyone seemed to have been waiting for their little tête-à-tête to end. Then, as Rachel entered the main gallery, all the conversations kicked in.

Like they were playing roles during her visit.

She noticed that young woman again, her face still reflecting alarm, worry—looking intently at Rachel. She quickly looked away.

That girl knows something, Rachel thought.

And as Rachel walked out, she had this other thought.

Such a big building. And the gallery was tiny. What secrets did it hide?

Dr. Whitney said Martina was lost. One could probably get lost in the giant loft space.

And Rachel wished she could see it.

And as soon as she thought that, she knew it was something that—somehow—she'd have to do.

She walked out of the gallery.

The plane rocked back and forth with crazy abandon now. The flight attendant had been able to crawl to the businessman and get him in his seat and fasten his seat belt.

Now everyone was strapped in for the ride of their life.

But Alex watched her laptop, watched the image of the Devourer of the Dead change . . . morphing into . . . Martina. Her face so sweet, pretty, intelligent where once the jackal-like creature had been.

How did that happen? Did something make the other file pop up? That must be—

And then—she heard a voice.

It didn't seem to come from the laptop. No, the voice sounded as though it were in her ears, as if she were wearing earphones.

"Help me," the voice whispered. In response, the plane bounced a few times like a speedboat hitting three-foot chop. Alex looked at the face on the screen.

The eyes blinked.

"I can't breathe here. There's nothing to breathe here."

Alex grabbed the armrests of the seat harder.

Tears appeared at the eyes of Martina's image. Tears, and actual droplets of water appeared on the screen. They started to run down the screen, turning from clear to blood-red.

The plane shook sharply left and right.

It occurred to Alex that she could hear this voice despite all the screams, the terrifying din that filled the cabin.

Alex wanted to say something to the image, maybe ask it a question.

"Where are you? How can we—"

The image started to fade. One more time the voice whispered. "Save me . . ." And as the image faded, it was replaced with what looked like a swirling sea, churning, foamy—only with each jagged spit of foamy water, the moving image turned more crimson, until it was a bloodred sea.

The plane hit another bump in the air and now the notebook, which had seemed somehow protected, flew to the floor with a sickening thud.

And then—

There were no more bumps.

Farrand was deeply asleep but he stirred to wakefulness when he felt a touch on his arm.

"Jerry, you okay?"

Farrand blinked. "Oh, yes. Could I have—" he craned his head to look around "—my glasses?"

Father Murray gave him his glasses.

"I've been asleep a long time?"

The priest smiled. "Very long time. It's late and you slept

most of the day. We want you to have some food. See how you feel."

Farrand nodded.

"I feel . . . okay, I think. A bit hungry."

"Traditional English breakfast sound okay?"

Farrand laughed. "Haven't had one of those in years. Sounds great."

"Good. It will be up soon. Some coffee, juice, too."

There was a pause. Farrand thought that Father Murray must be wondering how he got so lucky to have this crazy ex-priest show up on his doorstep.

"Look, Tom . . . I'm sorry. About last night. I understand—"

Father Murray put up a hand.

"Look, last night I didn't know what to make of your story. But that's changed."

"Changed?"

"Yes. The police released some of the details . . . of the killing. The tabloids are having a field day. Apparently, it looks as though the couple on the farm were the victims of a multiple animal attack. And what kind of animal? The police haven't a clue. To quote *The Daily Mirror:* 'It's like nothing we've ever seen'."

"They'll want to talk with me?"

"Yes. But you won't be a suspect."

Farrand looked away. And then what? How long before they track him here?

"And there's something else."

Farrand looked up.

"I'm going to try and help you."

"You mean you believe my story?"

"I don't know what I believe. But this is way beyond my ability to deal with. Some people got killed, you might be next. I put calls in to colleagues in the United States and the continent." Father Murray laughed. "You wouldn't believe how hard it was to explain what I might be looking for—even I don't know. But one contact up at the Vatican, he's a writer and psychologist, said he had an idea of something that might help."

"And that is—"

"He wanted to check and get back to me. Should be soon now. So, let's get some breakfast into you, invite the police over, and then we'll see what we can do to help."

A knock on the door.

"Hope your arteries are ready for some good old English cholesterol."

"Can't wait," Farrand said.

Everything felt slightly dreamlike as Rachel walked down Spring to Broadway.

I wish Greg were here, she thought. So lonely . . . surrounded by all these people.

No, she knew it was more than that.

The gallery, the ancient artifacts and the way all the people stopped and watched—as if they were display items. It was freaky.

And though she didn't think that she had much in the way of intuition, she felt that something was wrong with Dr. Whitney, with that gallery, with the whole thing. Some of the answers might lie in the building itself.

And how are my breaking-in skills?

Nonexistent.

She dug out her cell phone and called her hotel, accessing her voice mail.

She heard a cheery female voice say: "You have three new messages."

She pressed 7 to access the first message.

"Rachel, Derek here. Tried to reach you this morning. Guess you are out. Alex arrives a little after six and will go directly from Kennedy to your hotel. Call when you get this."

Rachel looked around. The message annoyed her. She always had this lingering feeling that Derek and the others didn't think she had what it takes to be a full-fledged member of the Legacy. Nick even said to her once, "You're too much the scientist."

To which Rachel answered, "You could all use a little more science."

Now Alex was coming out. To help, to supervise.

It was . . . annoying.

She listened to the next message.

"Hi, Rachel, it's Greg. Look, this damned meeting is going to drag through dinner. Can we hook up at your hotel . . . say eight or so? We can have a drink and see what you've found out. See you then."

Funny, she barely knew Greg, but she liked him. Of course, as one of her newly divorced friends might say, what's not to like.

Then the last message.

Derek again, sounding alarmed.

"Rachel, still haven't heard from you. Please call me. Alex is due there in a few hours. Bye."

Come on, Rachel thought. *Trust me, Derek. I'm a grown-up. I know what I'm doing here.* She closed the cell phone and slipped it into her purse.

Someone grabbed her arm. Rachel spun around. If it was a purse snatcher he'd get a quick knee in the groin. Time to see if those kickboxing lessons pay off.

But when she spun around she saw a young woman from the gallery, the one who had looked so concerned. Her black hair was cut short. Her eyes, also dark, looked terrified.

"Keep walking," she said. When Rachel didn't immediately move, she hissed. "Please. Before they see."

"Before who sees?"

"*Please.* Just keep walking."

Past Greene Street, and the young woman steered Rachel ahead by her elbow.

"Look," Rachel said. "I don't know what you are doing—"

"Please." The woman sounded like a little girl. Scared in the dark.

Faster now, until they reached Broadway. The girl ignored the red light and had them dodging cars as they ran across. She looked over her shoulder and, by instinct, Rachel looked too. She saw a swarm of SoHo hipsters.

What's going on? Rachel wondered.

But if the gallery has something to do with Martina's disappearance, then it can't hurt to talk.

"You can let go of my elbow," Rachel said.

The girl freed her.

The girl was nearly running, now moving past the trendy bistro, Balthazar with its stacks of French bread lined up appealingly in the window.

I could use dinner, Rachel thought.

She imagined . . . maybe . . . she and Greg, some quiet place.

Got to rein in those romantic impulses.

Further down the street, and the girl cut across the corner of Crosby, down a street where the exposed cobblestone looked as though they were rocks in a stream of asphalt.

"Can I ask where we're going?"

"No," the girl said.

Up the block. Now there was no hip throng behind them and when Rachel looked over her shoulder, she was genuinely concerned to see a nearly empty street. A few lonely, Hopper-esque figures stood down on the corner. In the early shadows of a New York sunset, they looked ominous.

The girl stopped.

"In here," she said.

Rachel looked left.

It was hard to tell what exactly "here" was. There were books in the window, but she also saw tables inside, and what looked like the balcony of a library.

Rachel took a step back to read the sign.

"The Used Book Café?"

The girl looked right and left. "Please, come in now." Then she looked right at Rachel. "If you want to see Martina again."

THIRTEEN

Rattus rattus...

That was the full name for the common American rat, which was actually a European import. The rat was an incredible creature, Nick was learning as he studied dozens of Websites and scientific pages devoted to the rodent.

Rats could gnaw through just about anything, even metal. They could eat just about anything that even remotely resembled food. They bred in large numbers, lived together, and could quickly infest a welcoming environment, and their definition of welcoming was quite liberal.

But the real forte of *Rattus rattus* was what they could do with their body.

To enter a space all a rat had to do was fit its head in. If the head fit, the rat could squirm and wiggle the rest of its body into any opening.

And what about using cats?

A good-sized rat would leave a cat with an eye dangling from threads.

That was the other thing... eyes. Rats have lousy eyesight. So they tend to hug walls, traveling the straight lines of a house, up and down, left and right, using smell and whiskers to guide them.

That, at least, helped the exterminators. They could put little boxes of poisonous bait in the path of a rat and the creature would move into it, eat, and then, in a few minutes start to feel really bad.

The poison worked in an interesting way. The rat's stomach started contracting just as it felt this incredible thirst. It would—in theory—reverse course, and head for the nearest remembered water source. Oh, yeah, rats were smart—they had a good memory.

Once the rat reached a water source, the rat would just keep drinking trying to assuage this implacable thirst, drinking and drinking, all the time filling their stomach which was, by this time, hemorrhaging from internal bleeding and the influx of water.

Soon, the rat would explode.

Of course if you had a dumb rat you could easily end up with it stuck in the walls or under the floorboards of your house, guaranteeing a foul, ripe smell for weeks to come.

So, thought Nick. *That was the rat.* He already had pages on the behavior of sharks, enough to know that not only was that tiger attack all wrong, but the behavior of the hammerheads was even more bizarre.

But the one thing he hoped to find he didn't.

He hoped to discover some religious or supernatural connections with either animal, each an efficient little bastard in its own right. But there was nothing. Not like the hundreds of citations pointing out the religious and mythical roles of eagles, alligators, snakes, cats, you name it.

Nothing about sharks and rats.

Which made Nick question . . .

Was what happened supernatural?

Derek was convinced. As was Philip. And speaking of Philip, where was he? Everyone was mobilized to do something, but where the hell was the padre?

Screw him, thought Nick.

Who needs him?

• • •

"Good shot, Father!"

Philip watched his ball go swoosh through the hoop and then ran over to his partner in the four-man game, Raoul—a gang member and one great foul shooter.

"If I wasn't a man of the cloth I'd be an NBA superstar," Philip said.

"Oh sure! Right! If you were about a foot taller," Raoul said.

Raoul tossed the ball to one of the other team members to take out, dodging Philip's clumsy attempt to steal.

What does this say? Philip thought. *Taking time to hack around with the basketball. Am I saying that this game is important? Or that the kids are? Or the day-to-day street life?*

Or maybe, all of it's important.

Raoul snatched the ball and fired it at Philip for another shot, this one from farther away. Philip wheeled around and fired the ball to the netless hoop. This time the ball hit the rim and rolled around before finally dropping in.

Raoul ran up to Philip, two high-fives at the ready.

"My man!"

Philip slapped both hands. They were ahead and the other team stood there, watching the slaps with exaggerated disdain.

Philip threw the ball to one of the other team. This felt so good, this daily life in the parish. Working with the poor, the sick, the young kids, and the everyday churchgoers . . . Lots of little candles in the wind.

Philip heard a beep. He looked down to his pager.

One of the other players lobbed the ball over Raoul's head, and then his teammate slam-dunked it.

"Yo, Father! What's with that?" Raoul said, taking no care to hide his annoyance.

Philip held up a hand while he pried his pager off his belt. He checked the number.

It was Derek. The Legacy.

It's like trying to leave the Mafia, he thought.

131

"Gotta go," Philip said, turning away, ignoring the groans.

.For a while, it seemed as though the cockpit crew might have considered an early landing, putting down at O'Hare.

First, they said that they were considering doing just that. Then they said that they would make a final decision after the flight crew did a thorough check on all the passengers.

Amazingly, no one was seriously hurt. A few bumps and bruises, but nothing that required serious medical attention. Even Mr. Martini across the aisle only had an egg-sized lump on his forehead. Probably all the vodka kept him suitably flexible and anesthetized.

The pilot came on after the check of the passengers.

"Folks, since everyone seems okay, we're going to keep heading on into Kennedy."

Cheers from everyone aboard. Nobody wanted to be stranded in Chicago, certainly not Alex. She wanted to get to a phone and tell Derek . . . what she had seen.

She couldn't do it here, but she had to tell Derek that now she, too, was part of what's going on.

But what did the words of Martina mean?

I can't breathe here . . .

Where is here?

Her notebook was a mess. *Good excuse to upgrade,* she thought.

The plane sailed smoothly on, with no hint of the recent madness over the Rockies. Passengers fell asleep . . . except for Alex.

The girl guided Rachel to the back of the Used Book Café.

The place looked ideal for plotting the overthrow of the government, complete with inexpensive soup and sandwiches and a hodgepodge of chairs and tables that were almost defiantly mismatched.

"Starbucks this isn't."

The girl looked around. "Do you want something, coffee,

132

tea? They'd like you to buy something if you're going to sit."

Rachel nodded. "Okay . . ." The counterman, incredibly gaunt with serious eyes that looked like they hadn't heard a good joke in a long time, waited for their order. "An herbal tea," Rachel said to him.

"Make it two," the girl added.

"Blackberry, currant tea, boysenberry, jasmine, lemon, ginkgo—"

The list didn't seem to have any end. "Blackberry sounds nice."

"Me, too," the girl added. The counterman fixed the teas and the girl stood there, nervously looking around, saying nothing. Rachel figured that she wanted to wait until they were alone.

The steaming teas appeared, and they carried them over to a table tucked under the second-floor overhang. On either side they were surrounded by bookshelves filled with used books all looking for new homes. The chairs for the table looked like vintage 1955 kitchen chairs—albeit from four different kitchens.

Rachel sat down and looked at the girl who was blowing on her tea.

"So. Here we are."

The girl looked up, and then—still on guard—again around the room. But this haven for the readers and nearly homeless was empty.

"Business is kind of slow here."

The girl nodded.

"And you are . . . ?" Rachel asked.

"Sylvie." The girl blew on the tea again, and then took a sip.

"And you wanted to speak with me?"

The girl shook her head. "No. I wanted to warn you."

Another sip of the scalding blackberry tea.

"Warn me about what?"

Sylvie leaned forward. "It's like this. That—bitch, she knows what happened to Martina. I'm sure of it."

"What makes you say that?"

133

"See, she found out that Martina learned something the gallery was doing . . . something wrong."

"Wrong? You mean illegal."

Sylvie shook her head. "No way. Not illegal, well, maybe. But something else. They're up to weird stuff in that gallery."

Rachel hazarded the fist sip of her tea, still scalding.

"Such as?"

"I don't know. I just do wage slave stuff there. But I heard them talking and arguing. And Martina, she like, changed . . . she looked scared."

"How did she change, Sylvie?"

The young girl scanned the room. Her paranoia radar was operating at full throttle.

"You think we were followed?" Rachel asked.

"If they knew I was talking to you I'd be dead. Look, Martina isn't the first."

Rachel paused in mid-sip.

"What do you mean?"

"What I said. There was at least one person before Martina who vanished."

"And who was that?"

"This boy. Cute, had lots of tattoos. And he told me that he thought Dr. Whitney and some of her 'associates' were up to weirdness."

"And he disappeared?"

"They said he left for Seattle, that he was going to look up some friends who were working for some indie film company. But he never said good-bye to me! We were like real buds. And he never called or sent a card or anything."

She took a sip of tea. Rachel waited.

"Anything else?"

"Well, before he left for 'Seattle,' Jim told me something. He said he went to the upper floors and saw something that convinced him that Dr. Whitney was doing something dangerous. Maybe it was like a coven or something, he said. Jim said he was going to find out what it was. Then—he was gone."

The Used Book Café wasn't empty anymore. An old

couple in iridescent running gear ordered coffee while a nearby obese man whose glasses were about to bungee jump off his nose scanned the shelves across the room.

They still had their privacy—for now.

"You think Martina—"

"I know something happened to her. But I don't know what. I only know . . . I'm outta there."

"What?"

"They don't know it—but I'm not coming back. They'll probably hunt me down, make me disappear, too . . ." Sylvie dug in a pocket. "But that's why I wanted to find you. You're trying to find Martina and this—" she threw a plastic card onto the table—"will help you."

Rachel picked it up.

"What is it?"

"My electronic passkey. It will get you into the gallery and the warehouse. But you have to use it tonight because once they know I'm gone, it will be a piece of dead plastic."

"You mean, go in—?"

"Right. There are answers in that building, somewhere in the creepy storeroom. Jim found something out, maybe you can, too." Sylvie smiled. "I only know that I'm done with it." She smiled. "I am outta that place!"

Rachel looked at the plastic.

"This will get me in?"

"If you have my password."

"Which is?"

Sylvie's smile broadened.

"Fuck. F-U-C-K. So easy to remember, hmm?"

FOURTEEN

Rachel called Greg's office. The phone rang a half a dozen times before voice mail kicked in.

He was supposed to be there. Was he on his way to her hotel?

She dialed his cell phone number until—*shit, again*—voice mail kicked in. This time she left a message.

"Greg, it's Rachel. I spoke to someone at the gallery, someone who knew Martina." Rachel looked around. Was she picking up the paranoia bug from Sylvie? No one noticed her chatting on the corner of Spring and Broadway. Manhattan was cell phone heaven. "But the key will only be good tonight." She took a breath. "I'm going to go in, look around. I'll leave my phone on. Call me."

She clicked off.

Okay, she thought. *I'm alone.*

No problem.

At least that's what she told herself.

Rachel waited at a place called Jimmy's, an upscale eatery passing itself off as a diner. She ordered coffee and a bran muffin. The muffin was the size of a cerebellum. *More muffin than a body needs,* she thought. She nursed the coffee.

Every few minutes she dug out her phone to check for a message from Greg, finding nothing. The hotel also had nothing for her.

She looked at her watch.

Eight-thirty. A good hour and a half past closing time for the Okthoro gallery. Unless nice Dr. Whitney was working late.

She looked down at her coffee cup.

Half her bran muffin remained.

I could really use a nice slice of New York pizza.

Maybe later. As a reward.

She put a dollar on the table as a tip, got up, and walked out of the restaurant.

The streets had turned quiet. Spring down to Greene, and then farther east, all the old New York blocks seemed like a dank movie set after they've packed up the lights and sent the milling extras home.

The restaurants were probably still buzzing. But the dark, ancient streets of lower Manhattan had quite suddenly turned eerily quiet.

Even Rachel's footsteps—the clatter of her heels on the pavement—echoed, sounding like something out of a film noir classic from the late forties.

In fact . . .

This whole block could be something like the late nineteen forties, she thought. If it weren't for the occasional modern car that drove by spoiling the illusion. Still, the streets seemed to empty quickly.

Too quickly.

She kept walking down Spring until she neared Wooster—and there she slowed. She wanted to pass by the Okthoro Gallery building and make sure that it was closed.

She looked to her right as she walked by very slowly.

No lights on. The whole massive building was dark.

God, how am I going to see? she wondered. *Maybe I should go up to Canal Street, to Chinatown, and get a flashlight, and—*

No, that would take too much time.

Once inside, she'd just have to risk putting a light on. Who would notice?

She passed the building entrance; at the corner, she turned, acting as if she might keep walking north on Wooster. If anyone was watching her they'd see her making this strange U-turn . . . as she stopped at the other corner and turned back on Spring.

She walked even more slowly.

As she walked she dug into her purse, feeling for the plastic key.

No way she'd forget the password.

That made her smile. And considering the gloomy street, she could use a smile.

She slowed even more as she came abreast of the door. She looked ahead. Someone was walking this way from Broadway. And someone across the street, going in the opposite direction, passed her. She quickly looked behind.

Two young people, lovers judging by the way they walked glued together as one, holding hands, were right behind her.

Rachel went back to digging in her purse, pretending to be searching something.

Hm, is my mind in here? I must have lost it somewhere . . .

The lovers passed. And the figure that had been coming toward her had turned down Greene.

Spring Street was about as deserted as it could get.

She climbed up the nineteenth-century steps, dotted with thick opaque glass that could let light in from below—if there was any light.

No light coming from down there now.

She saw the card reader and slid the card in. Nothing happened.

Was the card dead already? She took it out, flipped it upside down, and slid it in again.

This time the keypad lights came on.

Okay, she thought. *Time to enter the password.*

She hit the numbers 3,8,2, and 5 . . . the numerical equivalent of the big F word.

She heard a buzz. The door popped open.

Rachel entered the small gallery quickly and shut the door behind her. She stood there for a moment before she realized that any passerby could look in and see her huddled against the front door, looking about as suspicious as she could.

She stepped into the shadows of the room.

There, that's better. In the gloom, she couldn't be seen from the sidewalk.

She looked around.

Perhaps a flashlight *was* necessary. She waited a bit for her eyes to adjust to the darkness. And then she waited some more.

I guess that's all I'm going to see, she thought.

She took a step, thinking that the gallery wasn't that large. She wouldn't have to walk too far before she found the door to the offices and the stairs to the storage rooms upstairs.

As she walked, she felt the presence of the ancient artifacts in the room. The bull-headed statue that, during the day, seemed beautiful was now an ominous figure, standing mute. The eyes on the stylized figures on the friezes seemed to watch her.

Steady girl, she told herself.

The floor creaked as she walked and the gloom deepened.

Where the hell is the door? she thought.

She turned around. A glass case holding bowls and cups from the reign of Cheops reflected the scant light.

She saw the door.

The inner sanctum, she thought.

She walked to it, twisted the handle—wondering what she'd do if it needed another key. But the door just opened and she walked in.

Alex stood by the phone in the new Terminal One at Kennedy. Crowds raced past her.

"Derek?"

"Alex. You've arrived. Good flight?"

Alex laughed. "Yes, one of the best. The plane was upside down for most of the time we flew over the Rockies. Look, Derek—"

People brushed close past her—and she waited until they were gone.

"Derek, something happened to me on the plane."

A pause. Derek thinking, Alex guessed. Worrying . . . *now Alex is part of this, too.*

"What happened?"

"The plane flopped around like it was a toy, my computer smashed against the window—"

"Smashed? Destroyed?"

"Oh, yes. But not before the last jpeg image on it changed. From the Egyptian deity called the Devourer of the Dead . . . to Martina Popov."

"God. I don't like this."

"That's not all, Derek."

"What?"

"The image talked to me. At least, it sounded as though it was talking. I mean, I could have been hysterical, after all it did seem as though we were about to die. But I heard it."

"What did it . . . *she* say?"

Alex quoted the words that she heard.

" 'I can't breathe here?' What might that mean?"

"She's reaching out to us, Derek."

"I know that. But why? What does she want?"

The gates had emptied, everyone off to fetch their rental cars, their luggage. All of sudden the terminal was deserted.

She didn't like it.

"Look, Derek. I better go. I'll get a cab to Rachel's hotel."

"The Four Seasons."

"Have you spoken to her?"

"No. I left a message. But I've heard nothing."

A door slammed. And a man in a blue cleaner's uniform emerged from one of the gangways. He looked at Alex.

"Look, Derek. Gotta go. Tell Rachel I'm here. We'll hook up."

"Right, Alex. And, Alex—you're part of this now. Take care."

"You got it."

And she hung up.

Rachel stood in a hallway. *Probably safe to turn the lights on here,* she figured.

She turned on the switch. Milky white light flickered from the overhead fluorescent lights. She quickly turned around and shut the door to the gallery. Then she looked around to see if anyone could see the light from the street.

No. It looked as though the hallway was secluded. And, she thought, probably the storerooms inside. She breathed easier.

She saw an office to her right. A small metal plaque outside identified it. DR. A. WHITNEY. There was a card reader beside it.

First Rachel tried the doorknob. As she guessed, it was locked. Doubtful Sylvie's passkey would do anything. She gave it a swipe. Nothing happened. She rattled the doorknob just to be sure.

Okay. It would probably be good to get in there. But how? It was a sturdy metal door. No amount of bashing would smash it in.

She remembered something she saw in a movie once . . . using a credit card to open a locked door.

Would that really work?

She dug out her wallet and pulled out her most maxed-out card. *This card should die anyway,* she thought.

But when she went to slip it into the crack between the door and the jamb, she saw thin metal molding that prevented getting anything into the thin crack.

"Shit," she said.

If the molding weren't there, she'd have a chance. She looked around the hallway. A trio of metal shelves lined the hallway leading to the storerooms. She walked past them, filled with boxes of stationery, FedEx supplies, giant rolls of bubble wrap. Until she saw a pair of thick shears. They looked like the type of heavy-duty shears she might use to trim her rosebushes. They must be used to cut packing material, she guessed.

She picked them up and went back to the door. She wedged one sharp tip under the molding and began to wiggle it back and forth. At first nothing happened, save the tip starting to turn blunt.

But then part of the molding began to buckle. Then a bit more. And with every little millimeter gained, a bit more of the shears slipped in.

She rattled the shears inside the bent cavity in the molding, wiggling the tip back and forth. Now the molding made a little groaning noise with every movement of the shears. And along its length it seemed to be separating. Rachel changed her strategy, twisting the shears side to side.

She was sweating. She felt the dampness on her brow.

Then—

She heard laughter.

She froze.

People laughing—so close.

The shears were stuck in the hole. She didn't move. A drop of sweat rolled slowly off her brow, down to her cheek.

More laughter. Then the crashing sound of a bottle. Then . . . silence.

The voices faded. It was just people outside.

She went back to finish off the damn molding.

Alex picked up her plastic room key from the person at the desk.

"Could you check for messages again?"

The attendant gingerly hit some keys on his keyboard. "No, I'm afraid there's nothing."

Alex had expected something from Rachel. She must have checked in with Derek by now. Where was she?

"Thanks."

She took the key and turned back to the glistening high-speed elevators of the Four Seasons.

Farrand sat up in bed. *There,* he thought. *I don't feel too bad for an old guy.*

Half of his turkey sandwich sat on the end table.

I could get used to this. I could forget about everything else. The only problem is . . . how do I live with myself? He rubbed the back of his neck. He had a constant pain there—nothing severe, just a dull, throbbing pain. *My new life companion,* he thought. He looked at the closet. It seemed so far away, holding his clothes. The pillow, the bed looked so inviting . . . it would be so easy to fall back, close his eyes.

He stood up.

The door opened. Tom Murray came in holding a tray with two steaming cups.

"More food?" Farrand asked. "I haven't eaten this much in weeks."

The priest shook his head. "No, some tea. We need to talk."

Farrand walked to the closet.

"No, I need to leave, Tom. I appreciate you listening, feeding me." He laughed. "And picking me up off the floor. But—well, I don't think I have a lot of time."

Farrand opened the closet. His simple clothes, gray slacks, shirt, a sweater he'd grabbed when he ran out, were all hung up neatly.

He grabbed them. He may need to buy some more clothes, maybe a bag. That is, of course, if he survived.

"What are you doing?"

"Tom, thanks for the sanctuary. But I have to go."

Farrand threw the clothes on the bed and picked up the shirt. He could smell his pipe tobacco on it. *Have to get a new pipe,* he thought. And in that whiff, he remembered that night, coming back to the farmhouse and then running from something that wanted him dead.

He started buttoning the shirt.

"Jerry, sit down for a minute, would you?"

Farrand nodded while Murray put the tray down on the

bed. The scent of the tea was sweet in the spartan room. A little jar of honey sat beside the two cups.

He took a spoon and scooped up some of the honey.

Farrand looked up. "I'm sitting . . ."

Father Murray grabbed his teacup.

"How could I guess that you'd take it without honey, eh, Tom? All those vows that we priests—and ex-priests—have to deal with."

At that, the young priest smiled. Then, as if he was casually commenting on the weather, he said, "I found someone."

Farrand paused with the teacup close to his lips. "You found someone?"

"Yes. Someone to help you. They're called the Legacy."

Farrand nodded. "The Legacy? I heard of them. Rumors of some secret group investigating psychic fraud and—"

"They do a lot more than that, Jerry. I had to move all the way up to the inner sanctum of the Vatican but apparently this group remains in touch with the Holy See. I tell you—they were reluctant to tell me anything. Or you, for that matter."

"Why, because I left the club?"

"No. They keep a close lid on any connections with groups dealing with what they call 'Unusual Matters.' There's a fine line between quackery and religion."

"The Legacy . . ." Farrand said. "And the Vatican has told them about me?"

Father Murray shook his head.

"No. In fact, the only reason they gave me the contact information is because I sent them the story about the farmhouse with a little of what you told me. They were . . . uncomfortable."

Farrand took another sip of the too-sweet tea.

"So where does this leave me?"

Father Murray smiled. "Alone, Jerry. With this one contact. As soon as you're done, I can arrange a call. They're based in San Francisco. You can—"

Farrand stood up again. He grabbed his pants. "No. No call. Can you imagine what that would be like? No, if they are able to help, I'll need to convince them that what we're facing is nothing less than the fate of the world. I have to go there. Now." Farrand laughed again, and shook his head. "An almost giddy thought, eh? The fate of the world! Down to an old man."

"Do you . . . want me—"

He saw the way the priest was looking at him. "Help me? No. Let me enlist this Legacy. If they're good enough for the Vatican to remember, that's good enough for me."

"Let me at least make the arrangements for you, the flight, get you some clothes—"

"That you can do. But do it fast, Father Tom. You know that expression . . . all hell's about to break loose? Well, guess what . . . it is. And I'll be damned—literally—if I'll let that happen."

And Farrand looked around.

"Now where the hell are my socks?"

Rachel stood inside Dr. Whitney's office. She turned on the light and, as the flickering fluorescent bulbs came to life, she saw a chaotic jumble on the woman's desk. A tower of books, all with Post-its sticking out of them, papers and business cards scattered nearby.

She leafed through the papers, which were mostly shipping invoices. The books ran the gamut from a two-inch thick history of Sumer to a mammoth volume documenting the treasures of Tutankhamen.

She opened a drawer.

The usual gathering of paper clips, pens, rows of staples.

She opened the lower drawer and saw hanging files trapped in some failed attempt to be alphabetical. Names of museums, names of, Rachel imagined, customers.

Another sound.

Rachel froze.

She listened, hearing the roar in her ears from so much stillness.

There! The sound again.

Could be outside. Someone sitting on the steps. A homeless person urinating against a wall—New York City didn't believe in public toilets.

She remained frozen. But there was no new sound.

What if someone came back in the evening . . . is this breaking and entering?

And she was losing hope that she'd find any clue to what happened to Martina here. It might even be exactly what Dr. Whitney said. Martina partied, met someone, and is probably off in the barrens of New Jersey.

Then where do the visions come from, the messages to the Legacy?

She rifled through the folders. She went to the M's . . . thinking Martina. She caught herself. No, not the M's . . . P for Popov.

But—

She saw a name.

A word on a folder.

Maroc.

No first name, nothing else . . . just *Maroc.*

She took the folder out.

Maroc, she thought. A customer, a location, a—

She opened the folder.

Papers slid to the desktop. Yellowed news clippings. A manuscript. A photograph.

She picked up the clipping. The Arabic writing was unintelligible to her, but this yellowed newspaper had a photograph of a ship and below the picture, the name in English. *Maroc.*

What is this, a sunken ship loaded with goodies from Egypt? Was Dr. Whitney planning an expedition to find it?

Intrigued, Rachel looked at the next yellow bit of newspaper, again in Arabic. But this time it showed what looked like an excavation.

Okay, she thought, *a ship and excavation. They go together.*

On to the manuscript.

It looked like some scholarly thesis. The title of the paper was "Reconstructing the Lost Books of the Dead" by Dr. Jansen Stafford. Rachel skimmed the piece, catching references to the sacked library at Alexandria and the mysterious death of Akhenaten. None of it meant much to Rachel.

There was a photo clipped to the back of the manuscript. The picture was turned with its back out.

She slid it off the paper clip and turned the photo around.

The face of Martina Popov looked out at her, a cheerful smile. Dark Russian eyes.

She almost dropped it.

For a moment she just held it tight, unable to deal with the fact that the ship, the excavation, the essay all were somehow linked to this woman calling out to the Legacy.

Slowly she slid the photo back, the same way, back out. She gathered the papers together and put them back into the folder.

Maroc.

She wished she could photocopy it. But she couldn't risk staying here much longer. And she still wanted to see the storerooms of the gallery, whatever was kept in the spaces upstairs.

She put the folder back. If she took it, someone might notice.

Took a final glance around the room.

Then Rachel walked out, heading for the stairs that led up to the storage spaces of the Okthoro Gallery.

FIFTEEN

Tom Murray went with Farrand to Heathrow.

Farrand looked around Terminal 3. "Long time since I've been to an airport."

"Yes, and they say Heathrow is an accident waiting to happen."

Farrand laughed. "Now you tell me."

"Too much traffic and the long-promised computerized control system is late. Well, you don't have much choice. They say Gatwick is just as bad."

"Wish I had time to take a ship."

Murray nodded. "And I wish you would let me call ahead."

Farrand shook his head. "No. I'm sure this . . . Legacy . . . gets crank calls all the time. Best I show up on their doorstep. I can be pretty convincing."

The priest smiled. "Tell me about it. But I will do one thing. I will let the Vatican know that you are going. I'll tell my contact there to expect a call from the nice folks at the Legacy checking up on you . . . to make sure they know that you're not crazy."

"Or if I am . . . then we all are."

The loudspeaker announced the boarding message.

"I better go. I hope I get an aisle seat. My old man's bladder isn't what it used to be."

"Don't worry. I got you a first-class ticket."

Farrand pulled back with a shocked expression on his face. "Hey, times must be good for the Society of Jesus."

Father Murray nodded. "Hey, chalk it up to millennium fever. Business is good."

"Yes." For a second neither said anything, and then they both started to speak at the same time, laughing.

"Good-bye, Jerry. And take care."

"Hey, Tom, good-bye—and thanks for everything. I'll let you know what happens."

The priest reached into his coat pocket and pulled out a small black book and handed it to Farrand.

"And what is this?"

"Thomas Merton . . . his *Thoughts in Solitude*. Seemed appropriate since you'll be alone."

Farrand took the book.

"Thank you. I've read it, of course. But it will be a great companion. And Tom—"

"Yes."

"You're never alone when you're with God and—"

Murray finished the thought . . . "We're always with God."

"Exactly."

Farrand reached out his hand and gave Father Murray a strong handshake.

Then without another word he turned and walked toward the gate.

Thinking: *I wish I felt stronger.*

And despite what he said, he also wished that he wasn't alone.

A fire door led to a narrow staircase upstairs. Rachel held the door open so some light spilled onto the metal stairs. Then she slid her hand on the wall searching for a light switch. After a few awkward moments she found the switch and the staircase became illuminated by a single incandescent bulb.

That's cheery, she thought.

She stepped in. The metal door closed behind her with a loud click.

Maybe—she considered—*I have enough. I got the name of this ship, and Martina, and—*

But I might not get another chance. I'm here now. I should just go up.

She started up the stairs, the metal steps making a clanking noise that echoed in the stairwell.

The stairs went up for ten steps, then turned 180 degrees around to the upper floor, and another fire door.

There was a card reader there.

Shit, what if Sylvie's card doesn't work.

She took it out and slid the card in. The keypad illuminated.

Good, at least it recognized the card. She entered the password. Imagine having "fuck" on your mind all day.

A click. Great, Sylvie was cleared to enter the storerooms. And her card would be dead by tomorrow.

Rachel opened the door.

And stopped.

She expected a hallway with small storerooms.

But this was one gigundo storeroom. The massive, towering shelves held crates and unrecognizable objects wrapped in protective tarps. With the light from the hallway she could only see the first row of shelves. But the ceiling went up for at least another story, and the shelves stretched back . . . who knew how far.

It wasn't quite the giant warehouse from the last scene of Indiana Jones. But it sure felt like that.

The Okthoro Gallery looked well-stocked.

But she wasn't taking another step until she found a light.

Not with so many odd shapes wrapped up like mummies. Probably statues and bowls, wrapped up to protect them.

Wish they had installed a clapper. Clap on . . .

She leaned into the giant room searching for a light switch. Maybe the lights were controlled downstairs. And

Rachel knew she couldn't face going back down and coming up again.

She was at the limit of what her nerves could handle.

She looked left and saw something catching the scant light that spilled in from the hallways, something metallic.

She felt it. A metal box of some kind. She felt its outline, then felt a little metal latch. She pulled and the metal surface—a door—popped open. Now she could see rows of switches.

She threw one. An area way in the back of the room became lit.

Another switch, and an area closer to her was lit.

She threw all the switches, and the mammoth storage room was fully lit.

Now, what the hell am I looking for? she thought. She took a step into the room, letting the door to the hallway close behind her.

Walking past the shelves that towered twenty feet into the sky, Rachel glanced at the tags affixed to the items on the shelves. Some bore the names of places . . . Addis Ababa, Tangiers, Bangkok, Cairo. Others bore the name of what seemed to be Egyptian pharaohs . . . Amenophis, Horemheb, Meritaten . . .

The objects themselves were wrapped tightly in cloth tarps or hidden in dusty wooden crates.

If there was a clue in this room, something to tell the Legacy what the hell was going on, it could take years to search through everything.

And she doubted they had years.

She passed another row. She heard a squeak.

Probably a mouse. No, scratch that. Probably a rat. New York rats were a species unto themselves, big and virtually impervious to the poison used by exterminators. Some reports she had read said that Central Park covered a mammoth network of rat warrens.

Another squeak. Closer. She turned to the direction of the noise.

Mouse, rat . . . either way, she didn't want to see it.

She saw it.

A rat. No doubt—with that head, and that snaky tail—it had to be a rat. And big. It could make mince meat of her daughter's cat.

The rat sat there, bold, watching her.

Used to having this all to yourself? Rachel thought. Then she wondered . . . what the hell does it eat up here?

Rats could eat almost anything.

But ancient artifacts?

"Shoooh!" she yelled.

The rat didn't move. Rachel stamped her foot. That at least made the rat move away, though it didn't exactly scurry. It just disappeared down a corridor.

Great, now I have to worry about whether it will pop out and surprise me.

Stupid rodent.

The rat was gone. She started moving again past shelf after shelf filled with items, any one of which could be a clue to what happened to Martina.

She stopped. *This is foolish,* she thought. *Hopeless.* She turned left.

She saw a sarcophagus at the far end of the corridor to her left.

The giant sarcophagus startled her, resembling a person.

The tall burial case had a human face on it, the eyes permanently open.

She kept staring at it. You'd think it would be in a crate too. Not out there, exposed like that. Had someone been looking at it, studying it?

She walked toward it, watching the wide eyes on the sarcophogus study her progress. She thought then of the clipping about the ship, the *Maroc,* and the dig in Egypt. What did any of it mean?

Closer, now the coffin was a mere thirty feet away, and she could see that the painted wood was still quite bright, the gold leaf—while flaked off in spots—was mostly intact. The painted arms of the figure were crossed at the chest, clutching the symbols of authority.

She heard a creak.

She stopped.

The rat again. Stupid animal. Then she thought, *Maybe there are a lot of rats in here. And maybe the later it got, the more of them that started to come out.*

She turned around.

Another creak. Not a squeak, not the high-pitched sound a rat might make enjoying its nightly prowl for food. No, this sounded more like . . . something opening.

Something like one of the crates, creaking open.

Then another creak.

Louder. The sound almost . . . eager.

She licked her lips.

She turned away from the sarcophagus where it still watched her impassively.

Yet another creak—followed this time by a thud.

Rachel's heart started beating faster. She could hear the rhythm pick up, the steady thumping building, the sound of the blood now roaring in her ears.

I'm losing it, she thought.

Got to get out of here. I'm hearing things. Imagining noises. Getting freaked by these noises—that probably aren't real.

Just have to leave.

Other sounds then. A scratching noise. She tried to place it. The sound of something moving, stopping. The tap of something on the wood floor, something like—

She remembered.

The sound her dog used to make when it came flying into her parent's kitchen hungry. The sound of its nails hitting the wood floor.

A dog sound, she thought.

She knew she wanted to run toward the door. But she hadn't moved . . . hadn't moved at all.

God, why haven't I moved?

Because now, with that doglike sound, there was something else, a dull noise, a slapping sound, something fleshy slapping against the floor.

And . . . and . . .

Rachel let the thought exist.

I don't know what that sound is.

She took a step. The sarcophagus watched.

Another. The door wasn't that far away. She could be there in moments, and out to the stairwell, and down to the hallways, out to the gallery, to the street, and—

Another step.

She heard a growl behind her. It wasn't a dog growl.

She turned.

She began shaking.

She saw the paws of the animal, and the long black claws that made the tapping noise. But it wasn't a dog. No, it had a long, sharply pointed snout, mouth open, teeth bared.

Glistening . . .

Then Rachel noticed the rest of the animal.

She saw how the sleek brown body, with its close fur, suddenly changed midway to pinkish skin, how the back of the animal ended in dwarflike legs, human legs ending in feet.

Human feet.

The feet that landed on the floor awkwardly, making that slapping noise.

She backed away while the creature tilted its head left and right.

Another step.

And then from behind, she heard a new growl.

No. God. Please.

She just took a quick glance over her shoulder and saw another creature waiting for her. The same long snout. The same truncated human torso at the rear.

The growls were in unison. She turned back to the creature in front. Its piercing eyes were locked right on her. Then the creature made a small jump. It seemed almost a test. A little leap forward to see what happens. The claws scratched at the wood. Rachel moaned, her own sound terrifying her.

More growls . . . to both sides of Rachel now.

Surrounding me.

She looked around for something to use as a weapon.

But the nearest shelves only held giant crates and more pieces wrapped in heavy tarps.

I have to run, she thought. *Have to get the hell out of here.*

She turned to the creature blocking the most direct path out.

I've got to pass right by it. That's all.

But the creature—as if reading her mind—opened its jaw. As if saying "try it."

Try to run.

On three, Rachel told herself.

One, two—

And then—

All the lights went out.

Farrand slept on the plane to San Francisco. He knew he'd have to be alert and awake when he got there. But all he could think about was a warm bed, a cozy room and hours of sleep.

I'm not up to this, he thought.

When the male flight attendant came to serve dinner, he crouched down and asked if Farrand was comfortable.

"Quite. I could stay here forever."

"Sometimes these long flights can seem like forever," the attendant said. Then the attendant stood up and moved along to another passenger.

Farrand looked at the cover of the book that Father Murray had given him, tucked in the pouch in the back of the seat in front of him.

He reached out, took the book, and opened it.

His eyes fell on a passage, one that struck home when Farrand first read it decades earlier.

There is no greater disaster in the spiritual life than to be immersed in unreality.

No greater disaster. *And isn't that what I've been immersed in for these many decades? Unreality. Fantasy. Unknown horrors. Unknowable horrors.*

And now that unreality is about to become real.

All the horror, all the terror . . . will become real.

And, Farrand wondered, *do I have any spiritual life left to battle this reality? Have I escaped this "ultimate disaster"?*

He didn't know.

He knew . . . so little.

He flipped to the front of the Merton book, and began reading.

The darkness was nearly total.

In that first instant she could see nothing.

Her eyes teared—in a flash.

Rachel became a little girl, locked in a closet. In those first few seconds, she was aware that the twisted creatures were still there, waiting.

But in those seconds, her adjusting eyes slowly saw that there was some light.

Must be a window, a skylight . . . letting some paltry streetlight in, or maybe there was moonlight.

She was shivering. It seemed she had spent so much time in the darkness even though she knew that it had been only a few seconds since the lights went out.

Then all four creatures began to growl. She heard their nails hitting the hardwood floor as if clawing at it. She brought her hands up to her face.

Move, she ordered her body. *Move. Run.*

She bolted. She could see the black corridors made by the shelves.

She ran and felt her legs brush against one of the creatures, first the fur, then the creepy feel of skin.

But before she went more than a few feet, she felt a pair of paws landing on her back. The paws landed with enough force to kick all the air out of her lungs. But she didn't fall. She kept running. But then she felt something far worse . . . teeth, locking on her ankle, then—

Biting down.

She fell with her arms flailing to break her fall.

Feeling as though the sensation, the pain, was coming from so far away, as though it was all happening to someone else. But she felt that snout close on her leg, the growl muffled by her leg—and she heard more sounds as the other creatures closed on her.

She pushed herself up with her arms. *Have to get up,* she thought. *Get up, get out of here.*

She smelled something. The hot, foul breath of something close to her face. The pain on her leg, the wound, was forgotten.

There were more pressing matters.

The smell filled every breath she took.

Get up, she thought, pushing with her arms. *Up—and—*

The lights came on. Blinding in that instant. And she saw one of the twisted half-human creatures crouched by her face, its maw curled into a snarl.

Then a voice.

"Rachel!"

She looked up and saw Greg.

"Help me," she said. But she made no sound. Her lips moved but there was no sound.

She watched Greg kick the creature standing by her face and it made a hideous wailing noise as it went flying. Greg quickly pulled her to her feet, and then kicked at another of the creatures, sending it also sliding on the wood floor.

"Come on," Greg said. "Quickly."

Rachel got to her knees and then, with Greg holding an arm, she struggled to her feet. He started pulling her out. With the first step, Rachel moaned. She looked down at her leg, open and bloody. She could move but each step sent a shaft of excruciating pain racing from her leg to her brain.

"Keep moving," Greg ordered.

Rachel nodded, and she looked over her shoulder.

The creatures, a pack now, followed them.

They got to the door. Greg opened it and moved them to the stairwell, slamming the metal door behind them.

He turned to her.

"Can you walk?"

"Yes. I think so. There's pain but I think I'm okay."

She heard scratching at the door, the nails digging at the metal fire door.

"Let's go," Greg said. And he guided her down the stairs.

• • •

Alex sat in the opulent lobby of the Four Seasons.

I'd love a drink, she thought. *Such an elegant hotel . . . could there be a better spot to sip an ice-cold martini?*

But she was waiting for Rachel to come back. And if she didn't come back? What would that mean?

That we—the Legacy—are all in over our heads.

She wished Derek was here. They depended on him so much, the steady anchor. Without him, it sometimes seemed as though the darkness grew closer.

Even here, in New York.

Some people came into the hotel, and Alex looked up to see if it was Rachel. But instead she saw a sleek young woman with boyish short hair dressed in the tiniest of black dresses. The gray-haired man with her didn't seem to be her dad.

Come on, she thought. *Where the hell are you, Rachel?*

The people at the front desk looked up every few minutes as if to check on Alex, wondering what she was doing. Waiting, watching—

The lobby door opened.

And Rachel walked in . . . no, she limped in, a cloth wrapped around one leg, leaning on the arm of a man.

Alex stood up. "Rachel!"

Rachel looked up and as soon as she saw Alex she burst into tears.

"What did the emergency room doctor say?" Alex asked.

Rachel sipped the hot tea that room service brought up. There was also a basket of rolls, untouched. She couldn't think about eating.

"An animal bite. They couldn't place it."

She looked over at Greg.

"You saw them . . . what do you think they were?"

Greg, at the picture window, turned around.

"Looked like . . . some kind of dog. Maybe—what did they call them—a jackal. At least half of it was."

"Tell me about the other half of the creature," Alex said.

"I've been doing a lot of research on animal symbolism in myth and legend."

Rachel nodded. "It was human."

Alex looked again to Greg.

He shrugged. "I didn't get a good look at it. I was mostly intent on getting us the hell out of there as fast as possible."

"Human? You mean it looked like human skin, and the legs, the feet . . . ?"

Rachel nodded. "It was . . . skin. But a strange sort of skin, like it was new, so pink. And the hind feet seemed shrunken, clumsily stuck on."

"And will the hospital tell the police?"

Greg came closer. "No. To them it's just a dog bite. We didn't tell them about the gallery."

Rachel saw that Alex looked confused by this. "Why? Why wouldn't you—" Rachel asked.

Greg sat down on the bed, close to Rachel. "If we told them . . . and they told the police, they'd go there."

"So?"

"And whatever chance we have of learning what happened to my sister . . . what may still be happening to her . . . could be lost."

Rachel saw that Alex wasn't sure. But Rachel knew only one thing. Greg had saved her life. She watched Alex studying Greg.

"Tell me, Greg . . . how did you get in? Rachel had the key—"

"Yes. But I knew she was going to the gallery. When she didn't answer at the hotel, I went there. Fortunately, she didn't shut the door tight. I walked right in."

Alex nodded.

Rachel said, "If you hadn't come, they would have killed me."

"Yes, you were lucky," Alex said.

"But that's not all. I found something about Martina. I don't know what it all means. But—"

The phone rang.

Rachel picked it up. Derek!

And it felt so good to hear Derek's voice

SIXTEEN

Derek looked at Nick and Phil seated across the big table from him.

"Okay, we're all set here. How about there, Alex?"

After his call earlier, he gave them time to arrange for a speakerphone to be brought to Rachel's room. He knew that Martina Popov's brother was with them.

"Yes, Derek. It sounds fine."

Derek nodded. "Okay, why don't you start—and then we'll tell you what we've been able to find out."

Derek heard Rachel describe her encounter in the gallery.

"God," Nick said, "this is getting too weird."

Derek held up a hand, silencing Nick. "Rachel," Derek said, "how are you now?"

"Okay. The bone didn't break—and while I'll limp for a while, there's no permanent damage."

"Good. Now tell us about the other things you found."

Rachel described the clippings she'd found, the essay, and Martina's picture.

Derek looked at Nick and Philip. They knew what he was about to tell the others in New York.

"Derek, I don't know what those old news stories might have to do with Martina . . . or those things that attacked me."

Derek waited a moment. *I don't like this,* he thought, *I don't have enough information. And yet—if we don't act soon, it may be too late. For Martina, and who knows what else.*

"Rachel, we know something about that ship."

He looked at Nick.

"Rachel, Alex . . ." Nick said. "That ship, the *Maroc*, left Egypt from Port Said in November of 1947. There was no indication of where it was bound, no bill of lading. Authorities were paid off, and then the ship and its cargo disappeared."

"Yes. So how does it connect to Martina?" Greg said.

That was Martina's brother. Derek was unsure about having him participate in the conference. But he saved Rachel, he wanted to help his sister, and he might be useful in New York.

"Hold on. We'll get to that, Greg," Derek said. "Yesterday I got a call from an old friend of the Legacy. A famous woman, an oceanographic cartographer."

"Callie Peterson?" Alex asked.

"Yes. Callie called because she found a wreck on one of the satellite scans, somewhere on the Bermuda Rise. And she was able to learn what ship it was. It was the *Maroc*."

Derek waited while the information sunk in.

"And she just found it yesterday?" Greg said. "Well isn't that an incredible coincidence?"

"No," Derek said. "That's just it. I *don't* think that it's an incredible coincidence. In fact, just the opposite. I think Callie got that image, noticed that image, because something reached out to her, like it's reaching out to us."

"Martina . . ." Greg said.

"That's what we think," Philip said. "Listen, Greg, was your sister religious?"

"Well, we were brought up Russian Orthodox. But I don't think it stuck. Not with me, certainly, and I doubt with Martina."

"Was she spiritual at all?"

A pause. "No. I mean, she spoke about her work—"

"Her work?"

"Ancient Egypt. The Egyptian social structure, the religious practices, the mythology—all that fascinated her."

Derek leaned forward. "Greg, did she ever mention anything about the Books of the Dead?"

A pause. And Derek thought, *Are we on the right track here or way off base?*

But after what happened to Rachel he was more convinced than ever that this was all coming together . . . the animal attacks, the *Maroc*, the Books of the Dead.

"No. I mean, not that I can remember. Books of the Dead—what are they?"

Derek ignored the question. "Listen, Alex, all your files are lost?"

"Yes, my computer was trashed."

"Okay, listen up. Here's what we think we know here. That ship, the *Maroc*, left Port Said in 1947. It contained artifacts from a new dig site, stolen artifacts. We think that one of those artifacts may be a portion of the missing Books of the Dead."

"I don't understand. How does this—"

"Hold on," Derek said. "We're getting there. Some group of fanatics, a cult, could have been trying to smuggle them out of Egypt to someplace where they could be used."

"God," Alex said.

"I'm confused, too," Rachel said. "Used . . . how?"

"The full Books of the Dead purportedly contained the secret ritual to connect with the other plane, to what the Egyptians called the 'Netherworld.' This plane was ruled by strange animal deities and humanoid creatures that wanted dominion on earth. They needed human help, but their ultimate goal would be elimination of humans."

"You're losing me," Rachel said.

"Rachel," Philip said, "we've been picking up lots of rumors about a cult that has survived the millennia, a cult that continued to maintain contact with this other plane. But they could only go so far, do so much."

"They needed the lost books?"

"Exactly," Derek said. "Now we know of this ship, its suspected lost cargo. And I think I have an idea what happened to Martina."

Did he really? Or was he just putting the pieces together in the most logical construction?

Why did it feel as though something was missing?

"Go on Derek, we're listening."

"In New York, Martina may have learned of this cult. She learned something that she was never supposed to learn. This cult had access to some of the rites and rituals of the ancients. But their goal had never changed over the decades—to recover the lost Books of the Dead, and let the others in."

"The others?" Rachel said.

"The gods," Philip answered. "Actually more like the demons. The creatures, the rulers of the Netherworld."

"Why would they do that?" Greg said.

"Power," Derek answered. "In exchange for gifts, like eternal life."

"Those creatures I saw—"

"Yes, they may be some crazed followers who think they are now growing close to some incredible power."

"And my sister?"

"Our best guess is that your sister found out about these experiments, maybe the cult's plans for hunting for the lost books. They did something to her—"

"But they didn't kill her?"

"No," Derek said. "I don't think so. And I don't think that we've been seeing a ghost. That vision is coming from somewhere. She's been reaching out."

"But where?" Greg asked.

"We don't know that. Maybe she was sent to some other plane of existence—to the Netherworld. Maybe it suited their purposes to do that."

"Purposes?" Alex asked.

As soon as she asked the question Derek could almost feel the tension on the other end of the conference call, across the continent. He had considered what they might have done to Martina. Like a zoo animal, they may have sent Martina there . . . as a specimen. He just felt one thing . . . she was alive.

"I'm not sure," Derek said.

"Derek," Alex said, "what about the animal attacks?"

"I don't know. Maybe they were trying to stop any contact between us and Martina. Maybe they were a warning. The equivalent of intimidation."

"And it's not going to work," Nick said.

"Spoken like a Navy SEAL," Rachel said. "Going to take on this cult single-handed, Nick?" She laughed.

Derek looked at Nick, so hot-headed. Sometimes he was more of a liability than an asset. But he was fearless, dedicated. Two qualities to be prized.

"Derek, can I lay out the plan?" Nick asked. "Okay. Based on what we think we know, we have an idea where these books, the papyri, might be. And there's a good chance that the cult doesn't—not yet, at least. If we get these books, then maybe we can stop them—and get Martina back. If we move fast . . ."

Was that true? Derek was anything but sure. He knew the books were key. But he also thought that there was a possibility that Greg's sister could be lost forever. Time would tell.

"You have a plan?" Rachel said.

Nick smiled. "Sure do. And I'll get some diving in the bargain."

He looked over at Philip who shook his head. "And guess who else is going with me."

Farrand's plane landed at O'Hare as scheduled. The cabin steward announced that he could get off or wait aboard for the next leg. But nearly everyone seemed to get off the plane. Farrand used the empty seats next to him to stretch out and sleep.

And amazingly, he slept peacefully, no strange dreams meshing reality and horror. He slept until someone tapped his shoulder.

He awoke with a disoriented feeling.

I'm in a plane. I'm asleep in a plane, and it's not moving.

The female flight attendant smiled at him.

"Sir, I'm sorry to wake you."

Farrand nodded.

"Yes, is there a problem?"

She kept the smile on. "Yes, some bad weather's hit Chicago. Actually extraordinarily bad. Heavy rain, winds, lightning."

Farrand sat up. His muscles ached from the twisted angle he'd slept at.

"So there's a delay?"

She nodded. "And we don't know for how long. I'm afraid you'd better come off the plane."

As if to emphasize the point there was a flash of light, followed by a giant crack of thunder outside the porthole.

"Yes," Farrand said. "Certainly."

He leaned down to hunt for his shoes. *A delay,* he thought. *I won't get to San Francisco for hours . . . maybe not until tomorrow.*

A storm . . . Is that all it is? he wondered. *Is that all that's happening?*

He slid out of his seat and followed the attendant out of the empty plane.

Callie Peterson put down two bowls of food for her cats. They wouldn't eat out of the same one. No, not her kitties. They were so spoiled they each had to have their very own bowl.

"There," she said. "A late night snack for you."

The two cats ambled up to their respective bowls and—after a sidelong glance at each other—they started eating.

Callie looked at the sink full of dishes. She'd been so busy lately that she had just allowed them to pile up. A few days of teacups, dinner plates . . . *I really should get to them.*

I was never much in the kitchen, she thought.

I have other attributes.

Then—though she promised she wouldn't—she let herself think of Tom. Her husband had been gone for over five years. She thought by now she'd be past it all.

But that hadn't happened.

Every day something reminded her that Tom wasn't here. The only thing that made that go away was her work.

Which I guess, she thought, *is the reason I work so much and clean so little.*

She wandered into the room with her computers. One was picking up the latest Navy satellite downloads, while she had left her big machine, her 400 MHz, rendering a new portion of the Atlantic Ridge. When her new map was done, it might not look any more beautiful than the old one, but it would certainly be more accurate.

It would be like having a magnifying glass on the ocean floor.

She sat down behind her main machine. A stack of color printouts was in front.

Go to bed, she told herself. *For once get to bed at a respectable time.*

Same advice she gave herself every night, same advice she ignored.

The computer in front of her was busy rendering, turning the satellite images into fully drawn pictures to fit into her new map of the Atlantic sea floor. She could use it for other things like checking e-mail—but that would only slow it down.

She picked up the pile of printouts in front of her.

She rifled past the first few pages.

One of the cats, the tabby named Mr. Fitz, meowed.

"You've been fed, darling," Callie said. But the cat only meowed again.

She came to the image of the ship, the *Maroc.* The satellite image had been turned into a neat photograph of the flat sea floor and the ship lying on its side. Was she right to have alarmed Derek? There was a time when she thought Derek and his group were crazy. But, as Derek said, all you need is to have the unknown touch your life somehow once, and it changes everything forever. When her best friend lost a child to some cult—and then regained her through the

Legacy, Callie pledged to do what she could to help.

Still, Derek would often tease her.

You don't really believe, eh, Callie?

And she didn't want to. Still, when she searched this ship, and learned that it could be the *Maroc*, it scared her. What was being sneaked out of Egypt in 1947 . . . and where was it headed?

She looked at the top of the printout, where the satellite information was displayed, the time of transmission, the exact coordinates of the targeted spot, and—

She stopped.

She flipped back to an earlier page.

Mr. Fitz meowed again.

"Shush!" Callie said.

And on the earlier page, she immediately looked at the top of the page. There was the time, a few seconds before the *Maroc* transmission, that was okay. But then she looked at the coordinates.

"God, no . . ." she said.

This couldn't be. The satellite moved from coordinate to coordinate, nice and orderly, scanning the floor.

The image with the *Maroc* was far away from the previous image.

What did that mean? Did something go wrong with the satellite? Did she somehow mix up the printouts? No, she quickly looked and they were all in order. It looked almost as if this image came from some other batch.

Almost as though it were planted . . .

She brought the image closer to her face. No, there was definitely something wrong with it.

There was no way that it could have arrived in the same batch as the others.

But it had.

No.

Someone sent it to me. And they sent it to me so—

I would call the Legacy.

God, she thought. *I'm being used.*

The cat meowed again. More of a howl. Callie turned and looked at the cat. Something was spooking it. Sometimes the raccoons got into the garbage, if she forgot to put a rock on top of the can.

"Just some raccoons, Mr. Fitz. Now you quiet down."

She heard a noise from outside. She turned to look toward the hallway and the front door.

Then she turned back to the tabby cat. "See, Mr. Fitz, it's—"

The cat was gone. She felt chilled. She had always lived out here and, for the past five years, alone. She was never one to get skittish. What could be safer than Nyack?

More noises from outside. She got out of her chair. She looked down at her desk, at the picture of the sunken ship.

The picture that someone sent her so she'd call the Legacy.

Have to get to a phone, she thought.

The portable was usually right on her workstation, where could it be? The kitchen? Had she been talking to someone and left it there?

She started walking.

No Mr. Fitz. And the black cat, Inky, she was gone, too. They usually haunted her legs, eager for food. Where were they?

She reached the kitchen. She looked around for the phone.

Funny how cold she felt, almost as if there was a door open somewhere, letting in the chilly night air.

As soon as she said it she felt the breeze, a small cool breeze dancing around her legs.

The phone was by the sink. She hurried to it. Grabbed it.

The number. She tried to remember . . . but no, she didn't remember it. She'd have to find her directory.

Not exactly a number she'd keep in speed dialing.

Carrying the phone, she walked back to her office. Her black directory sat on top of the printer. She entered the shadowy room, clutching the phone tightly.

She went to the directory, flipped it to the L's, and found the number.

She pressed the buttons on the portable phone. It made a small beep. Then another.

The battery was dead. *Okay, then I'll use the phone in the hallway. No problem.*

She walked to the hallway. And the breeze, the chill at her feet, grew stronger. When she reached the hall, she saw the front door was open. Only about six inches, enough to let a cat squeeze through.

I must have left the door open a bit—and one of the cats pried it open. That's where they were . . . chasing those raccoons. That's what I must have done.

Except—she thought of one thing.

I know I shut the door. I thought I even locked it.

She was shaking now. From the chill? She didn't know.

She got to the phone. But as soon as she stepped there she felt something at her feet. Something wet.

A little puddle. And even in the dim light she could see that it was red.

Just . . . call . . . she told herself.

She followed the sheen of the bloody pool, a smear leading to a side room, a living room she rarely used. She pressed the number on the keypad.

It was ringing.

Callie felt herself breathing heavily now, almost gasping.

Another ring. Then—no!—a message. She heard Derek's voice, asking the caller to leave a message.

He wasn't there.

The message ended.

"Derek, this is Callie Peterson. Derek the—"

The phone sounded weird. Weird . . . because it was dead. She looked at it, shaking her head.

She looked at the front door.

She felt someone there, on the other side of it. Waiting there.

I have to get out of here, she thought. *But not this way. Through the back.*

She hurried down the hallway, then turned left to her small kitchen. The water was running in the sink. *I didn't leave any water on,* she thought.

The microwave *pinged*.

There was something inside the microwave.

She could only make out an indistinct shape on the other side of the glazed door.

Go, she thought. *Just keep moving. Run to some other house where the phones work and they're probably watching TV, and—*

She opened the microwave door, and trapped gas inside erupted, spraying her with blood. She spat, the blood touching her lips.

Inside, she saw a mix of exploded fur and skin. Almost unrecognizable except Callie knew that it was Mr. Fitz. Now she gulped at the air as though she had her head underwater.

She was barely aware of the sink filling with running water, streaming onto the floor.

She took a step to the back door at the far end of the kitchen.

Her legs wouldn't move. She looked down. While she was looking at the microwave, something . . . had encircled her leg. It was a crusty, brown coil, more like a leathery rope, stretching from the hall.

Now she kicked, trying to free her leg from the rope. But the coil only tightened, imprisoning her leg until, with one terrible yank, it pulled back and sent Callie flying to the ground.

Her head hit the linoleum hard. She reached out to grab something to stop her slide as the living coil, the snakelike thing, yanked her back.

Her fingers reached out to a leg of the wooden kitchen table. But she missed it by a few millimeters.

And steadily, she was pulled back, more and more. She had this thought: she mustn't look over her shoulder back to where she was going. She couldn't do that.

Then she did.

To see a man's face.

Balding. Glasses. Like a young accountant hurrying to middle age. His eyes were expressionless.

His upper torso was normal. She could see that.

But below the belt line his shirt dangled over a seething, dung-brown mass that pulsated, alive. It was like a giant over-sized boil, ready to be lanced. The long snakelike appendage extended from the center of the brownish mass.

"No," Callie said, looking at the small dark eyes of the accountant. "Please. Don't do this."

The head didn't respond, it just occasionally glanced down to check the progress of its appendage pulling Callie closer.

Now that coil began the process of encircling the leg, coiling around and around, until Callie felt its wet tip around her hip, then more.

"Please, let me go," she begged. She looked right in the eyes, right at the human head. But those eyes would only briefly glance at Callie then trail down to follow the steady progress of the coiling appendage as it now completely encircled Callie's chest.

She shook her head, weeping. She thought of her husband, her life, her friends, a crazy jumble of life images went flying by.

The coil hit her neck, then circled around until the tip of the thing was in front of her face.

It stopped.

She weeped, and she tried to say things—but all she made was an inchoate mumble, a pathetic hopeless sound.

She looked at the tip of the thing through her tear-filled eyes.

Right at the tip, as it opened a bit. Opened, and then she saw the tiny teeth at the end. But like a magic trick, the opening *grew*, as if it could simply fold back and become larger and then even larger.

Until she saw that the line of teeth continued on, growing larger, deeper in the maw of this thing.

She wouldn't let herself think about what would happen next.

Until—so fast—

The snakelike coil pulled back and then flew at her head. Engulfing it, snapping shut so fast . . .

PART THREE

Into the Maelstrom

SEVENTEEN

Farrand walked up to the airline desk. People had been besieging the employees but now there finally was an opening.

"Excuse me . . ." Farrand said.

One of the agents looked up; a young Asian woman with tired eyes.

"Yes," she said. She smiled but Farrand could see the amazing effort that took.

"Is there any news about when we might leave?"

The woman looked down at her monitor. *What is she doing that for?* Farrand wondered. Surely people had been coming up to her for the past few hours asking the same question.

She looked back up.

"I'm sorry. But the weather is still very bad, and even once we get the go-ahead, there are so many back-logged flights." She took a breath. "I should warn you—there's even a possibility that the flight will be canceled."

"Could that happen?"

The man next to her laughed. "Happens all the time.

Especially in this airport, especially in O'Hare. It's the busiest airport in the world with the most changeable weather. Go figure."

Farrand nodded. The agents were just a few steps short of losing it.

"You'll tell us?"

"Oh, yes. If we cancel the flight you'll know."

Another nod. "Then what happens?"

They looked at each other. The woman answered. "We book you on the next available flight . . ."

Next available flight . . . "And when would that be?" The phrase sounded deadly ominous.

"Why don't you just take a seat and wait, sir. We'll let you know . . . as soon as we know anything."

Farrand nodded.

More time slipping away, he thought. And how much time . . . before it was too late?

Nick looked over at Philip, asleep in the window seat. A red-eye to Atlanta, now the short hop to Bermuda, all taking its toll. Good thing they weren't landing in Chicago . . . the entire Midwest was socked in with an incredible weather system.

It was hard to believe they were doing this together, Nick thought. Usually, they were on opposite sides of every issue that faced the Legacy. In fact, he thought that Philip's problems with Nick were a big reason that he'd left the group.

Now it was up to Nick to get him up to speed to dive . . . even as early as this afternoon if Philip felt comfortable.

It isn't a deep dive, and I'll be with him.

But it was the reason that Derek insisted that Philip go that bothered Nick. Philip was a priest. He could, according to Derek, bring to play the protection of faith on the dive.

That was assuming they ran into something down there.

And what were the chances of that?

Zero, Nick guessed. No chance at all. If the ghosts on the RMS *Titanic* didn't bother Bob Ballard in his little submersible, then what dangers could the *Maroc* hold?

Nick closed his eyes and tried to get some sleep.

Rachel heard a knock on her hotel door.

"Coming, Greg," she said. She walked to the door and opened it. But instead Alex stood there.

"Oh, I thought you were—"

"Was Martina's brother supposed to come here?" Alex asked.

"Yes. He wanted to help us plan. Probably got called to a meeting."

Alex looked past Rachel to the phone by her bed. "Doesn't look like you have any messages."

Rachel turned around.

The message light wasn't blinking.

"Yeah, he'll probably call later." She tried hard to hide her disappointment. They wouldn't have Greg here to help them plan. She was disappointed, but that was because she found him attractive. Too damn attractive.

God, I need to get a relationship, she thought. *New York City isn't the ideal locale. I need someone who isn't three thousand miles away.*

"I spoke to Derek," Alex said.

"Yes?"

"He wants us to stay in touch with him all the way— and not do anything without checking."

"You mean—like breaking into the gallery?"

Alex smiled. "Exactly."

"Don't worry."

"He said he'll keep us posted on how Nick and Philip are doing. We're just to keep an eye on the gallery—and see what they do."

"Okay then, when do we start?"

"We have plenty of time. They won't dive until later this afternoon. In the meantime, tell me all about wonderful SoHo."

"Wake up, Padre. Paradise dead ahead."

Philip heard Nick, and then felt a nudge. He had been so soundly, dreamlessly asleep. He rubbed his eyes then looked out the porthole.

"Beautiful . . ."

"Yeah, nice island. See the houses? All different colors. For some reason, they love color."

"The water looks so green."

"Yup. Good clarity, as we divers say. Not as good as the Caymans, but you can probably see eighty to one hundred feet on a good day."

Philip turned to Nick. "And today is . . ."

Nick laughed. "That remains to be seen. Weather looks . . . changeable. See?"

Nick pointed out the cabin window and Philip turned to see a line of dark clouds way off on the horizon.

"They look pretty far away," Philip said.

The plane banked to the left, flying over the southern tip of the island and curving around. Philip looked down and saw the small St. George's airport.

"All depends on wind speed, Padre. Winds pick up, then those clouds could be over us by late afternoon."

"I guess that will answer the question," Philip said.

"What question?"

He turned to Nick. "Whether it's a good day or not?"

And Nick laughed.

Rob Parker took a final drag on his stub of a Macanudo and then tossed the stogie to the side of his Land Rover. His Rover wasn't one of those new yuppie Rovers . . . he had the real thing. A vintage safari vehicle with more dents than he could count and the bumpiest ride from hell. But it went everywhere and never stopped running.

He had all the gear in the back.

Crazy thing this, he thought. A training session in the morning followed almost immediately with a dive fifty miles out, over the Bermuda Rise.

Crazy. Of course they came to the right guy.

Best equipment, best boat, and—if they were so inclined—the best weed on the island.

He watched the plane finish its banking turn and head in for its landing.

Who were they? he wondered.

What the hell were they doing?

All he knew was that they flew in from San Francisco. One diver was U.S. Grade A prime—a trained ex–Navy SEAL. The other was a total newbie.

What the hell were they up to? It wasn't kosher, Parker knew.

He guessed that there was money involved. Money, drugs, something. But why the new guy? Why give someone a crash course in diving?

It was weird.

He thought about lighting up a small doobie. Take the edge off.

Not a good idea. Not if they had a long day ahead. Plenty of time for that later.

The money was good. Shit, it was great. A direct transfer into his Bank of Hamilton account. Bingo. And like that he was two grand richer.

Still, diving was about knowing what you were up to, what you might face. Plan your dive and dive your plan, that was the divemaster's credo.

And I don't know shit, he thought.

He felt a breeze lap at him. Just a gust, but it was enough to make him check the horizon. He saw the thin line of black clouds, squatting far away.

But Parker knew: they're far away.

Stay away, he thought. *We don't want any weather today.*

And then in answer, he felt another gust just as the American Airlines plane touched down.

What time was it? Farrand had changed his watch from UK time—but then forgot the time difference. Was it five hours, six? No, he thought that would be for New York, and I'm in Chicago. So it's what . . . another hour?

But looking out the window told him that night had finally melted into dawn, still rainy, still overcast.

I feel trapped, he thought.

He wondered if he should go up and ask what was going on . . . but the steady stream of angry, disgruntled passengers told the story. The airport was now filled to bursting

179

with delayed flights stacked upon delayed flights.

I'll never get out of here.

Trapped in Chicago.

But not long after the giant windows overlooking the runways brightened with dawn's light, there was an announcement.

Farrand listened carefully. The voice on the loudspeaker was tired. It had been a long night for everyone.

But the voice said Farrand's flight number, then the destination, and then—God, yes—a departure time.

It was still hours away. But he was getting out.

Maybe it's not all hopeless, he thought.

One of the deadly sins, he thought. *Despair.*

I will not despair.

The rover bounced jerkily on the road while Rob Parker talked non-stop.

"First time to Bermuda?" he asked, turning away from the road to look over at Nick who wished he'd keep his damn eyes on the road.

Nick looked back at Philip, and gave him a "what's this guy on?" look.

"I dived some wrecks here about ten years ago," Nick said.

"Really." Another look away from the road. The streets in Bermuda were torturously narrow. They didn't let the tourists rent cars, preferring them to use the deadly mopeds. Better a tourist breaks his legs in a scooter accident than take out a line of school children with a rented Fiesta.

"What wreck?" Parker said.

"The *Maria Elena.*" Nick sorely wanted to ask the divemaster to keep his eyes on the road. But then he thought—this guy has lived here his whole life. Probably too early for him to be drunk—or stoned. Nick had spotted a roach on the floor by the gas pedal.

Okay.

Parker smiled at Nick. *Or maybe he knows he's rattling us by driving fifty miles an hour in a ten miles per hour zone.*

Testing our mettle.

They came to a cross-section, and Parker swerved left. The bright morning sunlight turned the palm trees and bougainvillea into an electric green.

"No way I'd drive here," Nick said.

Parker laughed. "The cabbies would kill you."

When the rover turned, Nick looked east and he checked the line of clouds. The cloud bank looked as though it hadn't moved at all. *That's good,* Nick thought. *Just stay over there until this day is over.*

"Are the Bermudians religious?" Philip asked from the back.

The good padre, always worrying about people's souls.

The question prompted a full swivel from Parker. Nick locked his eyes on the front windshield and grabbed the left armrest.

This guy is nuts, he thought.

"Depends on what you mean by religious. A lot of Church of England on the island. I mean, the ties to Mother England are pretty damn strong. But there are some Catholics, too. And of course, there are the local brews . . ."

"Local brews?" Philip asked.

Nick shot him a quick look. Enough with the questions already!

Parker waved at a cabby going in the other direction. That their vehicles nearly scraped each other's paint off didn't seem to faze either of them.

"Yeah, there are some local religions. Little pockets of . . . hell, I don't know what you call it. Some form of Santeria, I guess? Maybe voodoo. A lot of the people go to a church on Sunday but also hit the local magic man for love potions or help picking lottery numbers." Another glance at Nick. "But good people. Good island. I love it here."

"I can see that," Nick said.

The Rover caught a big bump and the gear in the back rattled.

Nick turned around and saw the line of air tanks, tubes, and big yellow bags.

"You've got everything we need?"

"Yes. Exactly as ordered, chief. And I double-checked

my GPS. It was an expensive toy—glad I'm finally able to use it."

"GPS?" Philip asked.

"Global Positioning System. You give me the coordinates, and I can drop you right on the dime. Hell, I could drop you right over the *Titanic* if you wanted."

They hadn't told the divemaster what they were diving down to.

Was he fishing?

A new wreck could mean money.

"That's good," Nick said.

And for a few minutes, Rob Parker was quiet.

Derek stared out the big picture window that overlooked the bay. He couldn't see the bay, completely shrouded by fog. A dreary, lazy rain spattered the window and made the streets shine even in the dull morning light.

He felt so helpless, staying here when his team members were scattered to other parts of the world.

They're fine, he told himself. *They don't need me. Best I manage things here.*

Then why did he feel as though he was missing something by staying here?

He saw a woman walking up the street, her raincoat tied tightly against the bad weather, a black umbrella shielding her. If you live in San Francisco you're always well-stocked with rain gear. He watched the woman's progress up the hilly street, heading toward the BART station.

A gust of wind caught her umbrella and blew it back. The umbrella inverted and the woman was forced to engage in a comical battle with the wind, aiming the point of her umbrella at the wind to snap it back into shape.

Derek could see the woman's face now.

Quite beautiful . . . and lonely—

He got a flash of something then.

She just broke up with her lover. She's been crying most of the night.

The woman's umbrella popped back into position, and she turned back to bravely face the wind.

Derek felt something. *A flash*, he thought. *A little burst of something from that woman to me. It happens. Unpredictable, certainly nothing like the flashes that Alex can get.*

Just a quick burst from the woman. Her life, her loneliness.

Derek stopped.

For a moment the rain-spattered window, the fog-shrouded bay . . . disappeared.

I've felt . . . nothing, he thought. *Nothing. All through this there have been no images, no warnings, nothing at all.*

He turned away from the window. *Everyone else has been touched by something but not me?*

Not me. Why is that? Shouldn't there be something?

He walked back to the Legacy's Communications Center. Perhaps he should call them. Tell them what he just discovered. And—and—

Caution them?

Warn them?

He sat down by a computer terminal, hit a key and accessed the network.

No. No reason to call them. My flashes of psychic power are . . . unpredictable. This probably means nothing.

They have work to do.

Best to leave them alone.

"So, we go there and just watch?" Rachel asked.

"Yes. Nick and Philip will recover the lost books from the wreck—and we'll see what it tells us about where Martina might be, at least that's what Derek thinks."

"Yes, Alex—but what do you think? You're the one who's been doing the research."

Alex looked away. Rachel thought that she was holding something back, something she hadn't said.

"Alex?"

"Okay. I'm not . . . sure about this."

"What do you mean?" Rachel watched Alex pick up her teacup and take a sip, finishing it. She reached for the teapot and poured but nothing came out. "Want me to get some more tea from room service?"

Alex shook her head. "Okay, here's exactly what I mean. I don't know what we're doing. It seems as though, sure, we're following a trail. It all fits together somehow. Martina missing, Philip's visions, your discovery about the lost ship, the Books of the Dead. A nice package."

"So?"

"My mother wasn't superstitious. But she had an expression for everything. And she used to say, 'Watch out for any wind that carries you away'." Alex laughed. "I think she was talking about romance. Mama always worried about boys."

Rachel laughed, too—but then she saw Alex's smile fade.

"But that's like this. Everything seems to be . . . flowing, and not because of what we've been doing. Almost as though we're—I don't know—sailing on this sea. Something about it . . . seems so wrong."

"Don't you think we'll know more when Nick and Philip dive that wreck?"

Alex still looked unsure. "Yes, I guess we will. But I don't like this . . . I don't like how much we don't know."

Rachel nodded. "We'll know more soon." Rachel stood up. "Hey, I've got an idea. Let's do lunch down in SoHo before we start our stakeout. We'll talk some more. Sound good?"

Alex smiled. "Terrific. Let me get my stuff and I'll meet you in the lobby . . . in ten minutes?"

"Sounds good. I'll comb my hair and meet you down there."

"Great." And Alex walked out of the room.

Rachel sat there for a moment. This was still new to her; an incredible adventure dealing with fantastic things most people would laugh at. Sometimes it didn't seem real at all.

But Alex's words worried her.

She was not only smart, she had flashes of psychic vision. If she was concerned about the Legacy's direction in all this, then that was something for all of them to worry about.

Rachel got up and walked to the bathroom. She picked up her hairbrush from the expansive counter that girded the gleaming white sink. She combed her hair a few strokes and then grabbed the hairspray. She thought of Greg. He'd probably hook up with them later—and that thought felt good.

She picked up her lip liner and removed the cap.

Something fell. She turned around. Something fell in the shower. Probably a bar of soap, or—

She pushed aside the shower curtain.

She saw her razor lying on the bottom of the tub. She bent down to pick it up. But when she bent down she slipped on the wet porcelain floor. Her knees banged to the floor and she broke her fall with her arms slamming the edge of the tub.

"God damn." She quickly rubbed her elbow, trying to erase the sharp pain blooming at her funny bone. Nothing too damn funny about that bone—

She looked straight ahead. The razor was gone.

It was just there. She heard it fall, saw it, and now—

She looked up.

The shower head dripped, no steady drip but a slow buildup to a single drop of water that grew heavy then fell.

She saw her razor on a small shelf just below the shower head, sitting next to bar of soap. Right where she put it.

Rachel shook her head. *Did I fall so hard . . . that I picked it up and don't even remember—*

She heard a rustling noise. The shower curtain moved.

Get up, she thought. *Get up now. Something isn't right here. Just as Alex said.* She got to one knee.

Another rustle, and the shower curtain quickly slid behind her as though someone yanked it hard. Rachel felt the plastic brush her back, still wet from her shower. She turned, hurrying now, looking to see who was there in the room with her. Maybe the maid, yes the maid who didn't see her, she came and closed the curtain.

But through the milky white curtain, she saw nobody.

Her fist closed on the curtain and yanked it to the side. Hard. But the curtain didn't move. No, instead, she felt her tug rip it off the pole and the plastic sheet tumbled onto her. Only now—with the plastic touching her face, surrounding her head—it didn't feel like wet plastic anymore.

No, now it felt like a skin, a membrane.

It covered her face—and then, while she clawed at it, it grew tight, then even tighter, as though she was being shrink-wrapped in the curtain. Her hands went to her face to pull the clinging plastic, the skin, the membrane away.

She thought: *I'm drowning.*

Drowning.

No air. Nothing to breathe.

But the more she clawed at the plastic curtain, the tighter it seemed to grow, like a living thing, muffling even her screams.

EIGHTEEN

Nick looked over at Philip, then at Rob Parker, both standing in waist-deep water. The boat was anchored in a little inlet at the south end of the island.

Parker's face said it all: Philip wasn't a natural diver.

Nick watched him spit his regulator out.

"I can't clear my mask."

"Look, Phil, it's as easy as tilting your head back and blowing through your nose. And presto, your mask is clear."

Nick was steering clear of the dive lesson. Bad enough to give someone a crash course that went way beyond the normal resort course that tourists were shuffled through. Parker didn't need any coaching from the sidelines.

But the clock was running. And the line of clouds that seemed permanently glued to the horizon had started to change. They seemed larger, which meant that they were closer.

They still had to practice getting Philip down, practicing some air hose recovery, maybe some buddy breathing, the basics.

This is crazy, Nick thought. *As if a morning's practice gets anyone up to speed to do a one hundred-plus foot dive, let alone an enclosed dive inside a ship.* He was tempted to tell Philip that it was off. Screw Derek. He'd dive alone, or with Parker. A good dive knife is all the protection he'd need.

Nick heard a high-pitched screeching. His Iridium phone. The phone that can be used anywhere, even in the wasteland of Antarctica.

It kept screeching . . . probably Derek calling.

But there was no way he'd get to it in time.

No problem, it had voice mail.

"You know, maybe this isn't your day to dive."

Philip rolled his eyes. "Let me try it again."

And he slipped under the water. Nick stuck his regulator into his mouth and also slipped underwater. The water was wonderfully clear. The blazing morning sun sent golden shafts slicing into the water around Nick.

Parker slipped under. He was tubby for a divemaster, probably doing a lot of eating and brewskis in between dive trips.

Nick pointed at Philip and gave him the "okay" sign, forefinger on thumb.

Nick nodded. It was really Parker's job.

Philip gave him an "okay" back, and tilted his mask to let some water in. Nick could see the mask fill halfway with water before Philip let it again fall tight against his skin.

He waited. Philip tilted his head back, and then a great burst of air bubbles surrounded him.

When the bubbles cleared, Philip's mask was clear.

Nick gave him a big "okay," and then clapped his hands together, applauding.

And it really was okay.

He looked over at Parker. Time to move to the next step, racing time, racing those clouds . . .

Alex looked at her watch. Rachel had said she would be only a few minutes so she should be down any second.

Business people moved back and forth in the lobby, all with the purposeful strides of the truly busy. Alex felt strange, just standing there, waiting, and—

She felt something else.

It was as though a cold breeze blew over her. One second she was fine, and in the next gooseflesh sprouted on her arms and the back of her neck.

She gasped.

For a moment it was hard to breathe. She took another breath as though she might faint if she didn't get some air.

She thought of Rachel.

And she knew Rachel wasn't breathing.

She ran to the elevator just catching one about to go up. She hit Rachel's floor but had to wait while the elevator stopped two floors below that. It took an eternity for the elevator doors to open and a young woman to walk out, before the doors slowly closed again.

Some of the other people in the elevator glanced at her, sensing her agitation.

Come on, come on, come on . . . she thought.

Finally the elevator stopped, the doors opened, and Alex dashed out. She ran to Rachel's room and knocked. No sound.

"Rachel," she said. Then she yelled, banging full force on the door, screaming "Rachel!"

There was no answer.

I have to find someone to help, she thought. She looked both ways down the hall and saw a maid's cart.

She ran to the cart and heard the loud hum of the vacuum inside the open room.

Alex ran in and grabbed the maid by the shoulder, and the short gray-haired woman jumped.

"I need help," Alex said. "I need your key. My friend is in trouble."

The woman started shaking her head. "I can't give you the key. You should go—"

Alex grabbed the woman's shoulder hard.

"You can follow me. Go right to the room. But if I don't get the hell in there in the next minute my friend will die!"

The woman's eyes were wide, terrified.

Alex leaned closer to the woman's haggard face.

"Now give me the damn master key."

The woman dug in a side pocket of her uniform and handed a plastic card to Rachel.

Alex grabbed it and ran out of the room, racing.

The woman was probably calling security. It didn't matter. In a few minutes, if Alex didn't get into Rachel's room, it wouldn't matter at all.

She slid the electronic key into the slot but the green light didn't come on.

"Shit, she gave me—"

Alex yanked the key out. No, she had slid it in the wrong way. She quickly jabbed the plastic card into the slot. Now the green light came on and Alex turned the doorknob.

The room was strangely still.

"Rachel!" Alex screamed.

Still, no answer.

Alex wondered if she was somehow wrong, this feeling, this premonition.

She ran into the bathroom.

She saw a shape on the floor, unmoving. A plastic mummy. She knelt down and tugged at the plastic coating but it was too tight, as though it had been heat-sealed to Rachel's body.

And she knew it was Rachel's body wrapped in the shower curtain.

The plastic wouldn't budge so she felt around for Rachel's head, feeling it, feeling the mouth open, frozen into a gasping grimace.

"No, girl. No, hang on, please, Rachel, hang—"

She felt where her mouth was—and then, as though she was digging into a pumpkin, she grabbed Rachel's head and tried to press both her thumbs into the mouth hole, puncturing the plastic.

The plastic didn't give.

"Come on!" Alex grunted. To herself, to Rachel.

Come . . . on.

Until one thumbnail poked through.

Still no movement from Rachel. Alex leaned forward. She pressed her lips against Rachel's lips, but also touching the plastic. She felt the plastic sheeting on her lips.

She started breathing in and out.

How long had it been since Rachel took a breath?

Thirty seconds? A minute?

In and out, gulping air and forcing it into Rachel's lungs, until—

Rachel coughed.

Another cough and then a tremendous gasp.

The best sound Alex ever heard.

Rachel turned to her side and hacked at the cold bathroom floor.

With each cough the plastic sheeting seemed to grow looser. Alex peeled it away as Rachel coughed, and gasped, and then . . . after an eternity, turned to Alex, and started crying.

And Alex cradled her head there, while Rachel breathed in and out, back from the dead.

"You ready, Padre?"

This was it, Philip's test for his crash diving course. The three of them floated a few hundred meters offshore now, their BC vests keeping them bobbing on the water. The goal was a quick drop to the bottom, a mere thirty-plus feet, and then back up for a smooth ascent. If Philip could handle that, he might be ready to go down to the ship.

Right, thought Nick.

And if elephants had wings they'd fly.

Philip had his regulator in his mouth so he responded by making the "okay" sign.

Nick took his index finger and pointed down. Then the three divers lifted up their BC tube and "dumped" their air. Then it was just matter of letting the weights do their job.

They fell at different rates, with Parker lagging behind due to his extra buoyancy.

As the bottom neared, Nick shot the tiniest puff of air into his vest, and he slowed to a smooth hovering point a few feet above the bottom. He watched Philip crash into the bottom, sending up a silty cloud. It's what he expected. Buoyancy control was perhaps the most difficult diving skill to manage.

He kicked over to Philip but Parker was already there, popping a little air in the priest's vest. That's what Nick knew that they'd have to do at the wreck . . . get Philip as neutrally buoyant as possible so he didn't bump and scrape his way through the ship.

Watching Parker play with Philip's vest, Nick thought: *This is crazy.*

Nick hovered there a few seconds until Philip looked up and gave another "okay." Nick made a clapping gesture then pointed up.

You got down, buddy. Now on to the main attraction.

Parker gave a sign for Philip to go up slowly . . . hands extended, palms down. Nice and easy . . . watch your depth meter.

It used to be that a meter a second was considered fine. Just go slower than your air bubbles. Then the Navy found out that the risk of embolism was severely reduced by a rising speed half that.

Philip started up but Nick grabbed him and waved his vest hose in front of him. Philip nodded, grabbed his hose, and let out all his air.

You always surfaced with an empty vest.

Otherwise any air inside would begin expanding, and a smooth ascent could easily turn into a dangerous rocket trip to the surface.

This time, they smoothly covered the short distance to the surface.

When they broke the surface, Nick spit out his regulator.

"Pop some air in, Philip."

Philip treaded water, kicking to stay afloat when he should have been using his vest. Philip hit the air button and he suddenly started bobbing on the water.

"Your first dive, Padre. Congratulations."

And let's hope it's not his next to last, he thought.

Nick looked at Parker's ship, moored nearby.

Then behind it, he saw the eastern sky now determinedly gray, and growing grayer by the minute.

"Let's go," Nick said.

"You okay?"

Rachel nodded. Jimmy's, filled with escapees from office cubicles, echoed with the racket of clattering plates and utensils. It was the level of normalcy that Rachel needed.

"I told you, I'm fine. I'm okay."

"I still think you should have gone to the hospital. You were gone, Rachel. Gone."

She nodded. She knew she was gone, could remember only too well the feeling as the plastic closed tight on her face. It wasn't something she'd soon forget. When they called Derek he told her to go to the hospital.

Rachel surprised even herself when she said no.

Nick and Philip were diving to that ship, and what was going on in the gallery had something to do with that ship. If she checked into a hospital bed, Alex would be alone.

And Alex had just saved her life.

A young waiter, with multiple earrings and one ring clutching his right eyebrow, appeared by the table.

"Here you go, we got . . . one chicken salad on seven—count 'em—grain bread with the low fat mayo, and *una mista* salad with the balsamic vinaigrette dressing. And—" He looked down at the table. "Two more coffees?"

"Not for me," Alex said.

Rachel shook her head.

"Enjoy, ladies." The waiter drifted away.

"I still don't like this."

Rachel picked up her fork, speared a bit of the lettuce, and leaned close.

"You know what, Alex? Neither do I. But we're all caught in something that's trying to kill us. And walking away from that is not why I joined the Legacy."

"You have a point. But I have to tell you, Rachel. I'm scared. This is all too weird . . . and in another few seconds you would have been dead." She picked up her sandwich.

"For the first time since I've been with the Legacy, I feel like a pawn."

Rachel nodded.

And she had to wonder, *if we are pawns, what are we pawns for?* What is it that wanted her dead?

She had another thought.

What sent that message to Alex?

And why?

So many questions. And no answers.

"We'll finish," Rachel said, "then walk by the gallery, see who goes in, who comes out."

"Yes, and Derek said he'd stay in touch with the cell phone."

"Just hope your battery doesn't die."

Alex dug in her jacket pocket. "I have a spare."

"We may need it. And who knows what else we may need."

Parker had the boat running at full throttle, noisily hitting the waves and slamming down hard. Nick felt as if he was drunk as he lumbered around trying to lay out his gear.

"Are you shooting for the worst ride you can?" Nick yelled.

Parker looked back. "Did you say you want it . . . bumpier?"

Nick grinned. But when he glanced over at Philip, he saw that his partner wasn't wearing a smile. With good reason, too. The sea had turned seriously rough and choppy—and the more they pulled away from Bermuda, the worse it turned.

"You want bumpier? I can do bumpier! No problem."

And with that the dive boat seemed to hit a particularly nasty swell and slammed down in a trough that made all their diving gear fly up in the air.

"Hey!" Nick yelled. Philip looked positively green.

But when Parker turned around he wasn't grinning. "I didn't do that, Nick. The sea's turning real bad. Check out those thunderheads."

Philip repeated the word. "Thunderheads? Great."

Nick saw now the entire eastern quadrant of the sky was a dark gray, with an ominous curtain touching the sea— and that meant rain. And probably wind, and probably lightning.

The storm system was moving fast.

"We'd better turn back!" Parker yelled.

Nick looked at the gear. They were probably ten miles away from the destination. Turning back probably made sense.

"We're going back?" Philip said.

Nick nodded. "What do you think?"

Philip looked at the choppy sea, the clouds. "We're here." He took a breath, and Nick knew the answer that the priest wanted to give—but didn't. "And as long as we're here we might as well do what we came to do."

Nick stumbled up to Parker. "We're going to keep on going."

The divemaster shook his head. "I don't get it. You guys are . . . crazy."

Nick stumbled back to the rear of the boat. He opened a hard-shell case and took out what looked like a small space helmet.

"What's that?" Philip asked.

"My communications rig. A full face mask."

"Do I get one, too?"

Nick laughed just as the ship hit a wave and sent a spray of seawater flying back.

"Nope. But I can stay in touch with Parker who'll also wear one. It's a good idea when doing a confined dive."

Philip nodded and opened up a black bag.

"And what do you have in there?"

Philip took out a silver case on a thick silver chain.

"What is that?"

But before Philip could answer, the priest kissed the circular piece of metal.

Then he opened it.

Nick saw a small white host. He rolled his eyes.

"What did you expect?" Philip said. "Maybe I'd bring a water pistol filled with holy water?"

Nick laughed again. "Good idea—except I don't think that would work underwater. But, hell, Philip, what will a host do?"

Philip reached out and patted Nick's shoulder. "If a consecrated host can't do anything, then nothing can."

Parker yelled from the front.

"We're about five miles away. Start getting ready. I don't want to be out here any longer than I have to!"

Nick looked again at the clouds. *Nor do I,* he thought. *Nor do I . . .*

Derek sat in the eerie glow of the Legacy's Communications Center.

Rachel had almost been killed. If Alex hadn't gotten a flash, she'd be dead now. And then Rachel decided to ignore his order to go to the hospital.

I should go there, he thought.

A lot of good I'm doing here.

Once again, he had to wonder . . . *how come I felt nothing from Rachel? It's as though I'm out of the loop on this whole thing.*

He heard the chimes. Someone at the front door.

He spoke to the computer in front of him.

"Surveillance," he said.

The computer screen quickly displayed eight miniwindows, cam shots of locations inside and out of Legacy House.

"Front door."

One cam screen bloomed to fill the screen. And Derek leaned close to see an old man standing in the drizzling rain, his thin gray hair plastered against his face. The old man looked like a homeless person, glasses flecked with rain, looking around.

"Can I help you?" Derek said.

"Y-yes," the man said. He had a slight English accent but more like an expatriate who had picked up some of the inflection. "I was given your name . . ."

Oh, probably a nutcase. Somehow, enough people found out about the Legacy and they ended up coming here de-

spite the plaque outside which read THE LUNA FOUNDA-
TION.

"And who gave you my name?"

The man looked miserable in the rain.

"Cardinal Scigliano. At the Vatican."

Derek froze. Scigliano was a true ally of the Legacy. The
old cardinal had had some strange experiences himself, and
he understood the battle that the Legacy fought. Though
they didn't always agree on issues of spirituality, Scigliano
supported and helped Derek whenever he could.

"You met with the Cardinal?"

Derek wondered whether he should let the man in. If he
really was sent here by the Vatican . . .

But why hadn't the man called ahead?

"No. But another priest spoke to him on my behalf. The
Cardinal—" the old man took off his glasses, the lenses
dappled with wet drips "—said you can call him." The old
man huddled close to the speaker. "Call him. And then for
God's sake open this bloody door before—believe me—all
hell breaks loose."

Derek would call. But first he said, "Open Door."

And he watched on the screen as the front door opened
and the old man walked in.

NINETEEN

N ow the boat rocked up and down in the choppy water.
Parker had the throttle down, yanking the wheel left
and right, trying to keep the dive boat steady.

Nick, in his full wet suit, stood beside Parker when he
tapped the GPS beside the boat's wheel.

"Got you right over the spot." Parker looked around at
the churning sea. "God, never saw a storm front move this
fast," he said.

"Can you still anchor?"

Parker shook his head. "I can throw the anchor down but
I might as well toss it without any line attached. The sea
will just rip it off the bottom."

Parker turned to Nick—and Nick knew what he was going to say.

"I can't go down with you. Not if you want a boat waiting for you."

Nick nodded. "I figured as much." He looked back to
Philip, fiddling with the zipper of his wet suit.

"I know you might need some help down there. But I
can't do it." He tapped a speaker built into the boat's con-

trol panel. "I can still talk to you. I'll plug in the communications rig right into my radio here."

Nick wondered what good it would do to talk to someone who couldn't get down to help them.

"Great." He turned back to Philip. "Ready to dive, Philip?"

This was insane. Bringing a new diver down over one hundred feet. Totally insane.

On cue, the boat caught a swell that sent it rolling to the side, and Philip tumbled into the railing. When he looked up he said, "Couldn't be readier."

"Then let's dive before the weather turns even nicer."

Nick sat down on the bench beside his diving gear, slipped on his fins, and then pulled on the full-face mask. The mask felt weird since it covered his entire head. He hadn't dived with the communications gear many times— but he knew he didn't like it.

"Can you hear me, Parker?"

"Loud and clear." Parker's voice boomed in his ears. Nick fiddled with a slide switch on the side of the helmet.

"Say something again."

"Something again!"

Now Parker's voice—and his laughter—were at a tolerable level.

Philip looked ready, sitting with his BC and tank strapped tight, fins on, his mask giving him a startled expression.

Nick gestured to Philip to get up. Until he took off the communications rig, he wouldn't be able to speak to Philip.

He watched Philip sit on the boat railing. Nick gave him a quick "okay" sign and then checked that Philip had one hand on his mask and another on his weight belt. But the priest was ahead of him, already in the proper position for a backwards roll. A quick learner.

Nick popped another small shot of air into Philip's vest . . . and then waved his hand.

"Go!" he said, hoping it was loud enough for Philip to hear him.

And after a moment's hesitation the priest rolled backward into the choppy sea. In seconds, Philip drifted away, lost to the foamy whitecaps.

No time to waste, Nick turned around and fell backwards into the water.

For a few seconds, he felt that disconcerting, near-weightless feeling where there was no up or down. Then he bobbed to the surface.

Philip was still a good ten meters away. Nick raised his hand and pointed thumbs down.

Let's dive.

He hoped Philip saw him because he had to get below all this chop.

He raised his BC's release valve, let the air out, and began to sink.

"Are you sure you're warm enough?"

Derek took the wet towel from Farrand. Farrand smiled. "Yes, the fire is quite nice." He looked around the great room of Legacy House. "And this is quite a beautiful place you have here."

"Thank you. And your soup?"

"Oh, very good. Nice and hot, takes some of your San Francisco chill out."

Derek figured that eventually the man would tell him why he had made this incredible journey to see the Legacy.

"You know," Farrand said, "I had heard rumors of the existence of something like the Legacy. It had no name, of course. Just a rumor of a group kind of like ghostbusters." He laughed. "I thought it was just a silly story."

"As you see, we're very real."

"Yes. And I for one am very glad."

And Derek had to wonder: *Is this the best I can do? Sit and talk to this old man while my team is across the continent?*

"You're glad? Perhaps you better tell me why."

Farrand reached down and took a spoonful of the soup.

"I will. You see. I don't know what you have experienced, Derek. What . . . horrors you have encountered."

"Name it," Derek said.

For a moment Farrand looked Derek in the eye, unblinking, as if checking whether this was mere bravado. He held the look for a moment. Satisfied, he continued.

"Let me tell you what happened over fifty years ago. And then let me tell you what I think may be happening now. And maybe we can be of some help to each other."

He brought another spoonful of the tomato soup to his lips.

And after that sip, Derek listened to Farrand's story about what happened in Egypt; the find, the murders—and then—the disappearance of what he believed to be the lost Books of the Dead.

Derek leaned forward.

"Hold on a second. You're saying that you know that these books were found, and then smuggled out of the country, bound for—"

"Bound for, I imagine, the United States. They hold tremendous power. For the forces of darkness, what the Church likes to call 'evil,' those books might open the gateway to all-out war."

Derek looked away. For a moment he couldn't believe what he was hearing. This old man shows up on his doorstep . . . talking about the Egyptian Books of the Dead.

Farrand noticed Derek's confusion.

"Is there something wrong?"

Derek held up a hand.

"I need to know more. You say they were smuggled out?"

Farrand nodded. "Yes, on—"

"On a ship called the *Maroc*?"

Now it was Farrand's turn to react. "You know that ship?"

"Yes."

Derek saw the old man's eyes narrow. He looked even older, scared.

"Tell me how you know this."

"The Legacy has a network. We have allies around the world."

"Yes, but . . ." Farrand raised his voice. "How do you know of this lost ship?"

Now Derek felt Farrand's fear. A physical thing in the room.

"Because . . . the ship is no longer lost."

Farrand didn't move, didn't say anything.

Derek continued. "The ship was found by Navy satellites. We were concerned because of things that happened to my team members."

"What happened to them?"

"Visions. Hallucinations. Abnormal animal attacks."

"Where are they now?" Farrand's face was twisted by his concern.

"Where are—?"

"Your team, damn it. Where the hell are they?"

Despite the fire, Derek felt chilled. As if suddenly a giant door opened somewhere in the house letting all that cold dank air outside drift in.

"Two of them are watching this gallery in New York and right now . . . two others are diving to the wreck, to get—"

Farrand stood up. He moved slowly, as though his whole body ached. He came up to Derek.

"Don't you see what's happening?"

"Tell me."

"Listen. I didn't tell you one secret, something else that I learned that night from Daloul, something I never told anyone. I'll tell you—but first, can you reach your divers, can you stop them?"

The chill filled the room, icy, reducing the fire to mere light and color.

"I don't know. I can try. But why?"

"Listen to me and then stop them," Farrand said.

Rachel grabbed Alex's arm.

"See her! That's Dr. Whitney, the gallery director."

"She looks pretty businesslike."

Rachel shrugged. "I know. I don't know how she's connected to this." She saw two people walking briskly up to the gallery, a man and a woman. The man slid his card into the electronic lock and then entered the gallery.

"Know them?"

"They may have been there yesterday. There were a lot of people. I don't know . . ."

And then Rachel saw someone hurrying across the street. She kept looking—

Until she saw that this time she did know the person.

"Alex, God."

"What is it?"

"See that girl? I know her. That's Sylvie."

The girl hurried up to the gallery door, looked around, then entered.

"She's the girl you met, who gave you her card?"

"Yes, but don't you get it? She was quitting, that's why she gave me her card. She was leaving, and now—there she is."

Rachel watched Alex looking at the gallery, trying to understand.

"She still works there, Alex. They wanted to give me the card. Wanted me to get in. Wanted me to find everything."

"Christ. If that's true . . ."

"Then—somehow—Nick and Philip are being set up. It's as though they were being steered to that ship."

Alex had her cell phone out and punched the keypad. When Rachel looked at her, she said, "I'm calling Derek."

Rachel turned back to the gallery. She wanted to call Greg and get him to come, now.

Something was happening inside the Okthoro Gallery.

And she thought of Nick, Philip . . . a thousand miles away.

Philip saw Nick wave, as he rode the crest of a swell.

Must be time to go down, Philip thought. He raised his vest's release tube and let the air out. There was a moment's hesitation, and then Philip slipped under the water, pulled down by the ten pounds of lead on his weight belt.

For a few seconds he could still feel the churning water, the pulling and tugging of the surf.

But after a few more feet, things calmed as he slid below the waves.

It was just as Nick said . . . snorkel on the surface and you'll barf every time. But under the water it's totally calm.

Philip forgot to equalize in those first few seconds and he quickly felt painful pressure on his ears. He kicked with his fins to slow his plummet and then brought his thumb and index finger up to his nose. He blew once trying to equalize the pressure but he still felt the dull pain.

He blew again, and now his ears cleared. He slowed his kicking.

The water, even under the dark gray skies, was sparkling clear with great visibility. But he didn't see Nick. Was he still on the surface, looking for him? He looked to his left. Nothing but open sea. Then he looked right, and he finally saw Nick a good distance away and above him.

Nick gave him a gesture, which Philip took to mean slow down.

Slow down. How? Kick to stop falling? Put some air in the vest. Nick said not to do that. Getting the buoyancy right was no game for an amateur.

Philip started kicking but it only slowed his fall.

He looked up to the surface. The mirrorlike membrane of the surface seemed so far away.

How deep am I? he wondered. He looked at his depth gauge.

Fifty feet. And falling fast.

When he looked left again, Nick was closer, kicking over to Philip as he fell. Philip's ears started hurting again and he cleared them once more.

Nick came beside him and grabbed his vest. He found his air tube and shot a quick burst into Philip's vest.

Now they slowly glided down together.

He could see Nick's eyes.

I'm not alone anymore.

That was good. Those first few seconds of free-fall were terrifying, like vanishing down a watery rabbit hole.

Nick demanded an "okay" sign. And though Philip didn't

feel really "okay," he shot it back. Then Nick, still holding on to Philip's vest, pointed down.

Philip looked down.

And there, not too far below them, was a ship.

Maroc. Lying on its side, surrounded by a few rays, a big grouper as long as a kitchen table, and a school of yellow-striped fish.

Philip looked down.

And he thought: *We're going in there.*

TWENTY

Now Farrand stood over Derek, and he didn't seem quite as old. Derek even thought: *This is one tough bastard.*

"That night when I held the twisted creature that Daloul had become, dying, he told me something that I knew I should tell no one." Farrand looked away as though he was back at that moment, in the narrow side street. "I didn't tell anyone because I knew it was my only hope—our only hope."

"He told you something . . . ?"

"Yes. He said that before the ship left, he knew the horror it contained, the danger. And he did something about it."

"What was that?"

"He went to this old Coptic Church, more of a tiny room than a church. And he asked the old priest, an ancient man, to help. And the priest, an old friend, did help. He went to the ship and—standing beside it—he sprinkled the hull with holy water while he prayed for the evil inside to be contained forever."

"And you think it worked?"

Farrand laughed. "Sounds . . . funny, doesn't it? So superstitious. Walking around, muttering prayers, sprinkling
ordinary water. But Daloul and the old priest believed in
such things. And I came to believe also . . ."

Derek heard the phone ring. He was tempted to get it but
he had to hear the end of this story, to see if anything
Farrand knew posed a threat to his people.

"How was that?"

"The ship left . . . but it never arrived. Whatever was in
it never escaped. And I came to believe that it was due to
the priest's blessing. Something guarded that ship."

Guarded that ship . . .

Derek felt alarmed. What was Farrand saying?

"You see, Derek, that ship has been sealed. The forces
that want those books couldn't get them. And the power of
that guard has grown."

"Wait a second. Then you're saying that, after your attack, this 'movement' you felt, this sense that something
was happening, it had to come from—"

"You. The Legacy. Yes, I didn't know that. But now I
see." He took a breath. "The Legacy is being used to bring
up the lost Books of the Dead."

"This is incredible."

"Is it? Why, because you were tricked? They needed
help, powerful, committed help. Help that could break
through that barrier of goodness . . . who better than your
group, especially with a priest?"

"That means they fed us everything, the visions, the information—"

"Probably even the satellite photos."

Derek thought of Callie Peterson. Could she be in danger?

He got a flash. The first in such a very long time.

It was too late for Callie.

"We have to do something," Derek said.

Now Farrand sounded tired, defeated. "If it's not too
late."

"I can reach my team, stop them."

"Even underwater?"

"Yes . . . even underwater . . ."

"It's Derek's voice mail again, damn it. Why won't he pick up?"

Alex waited a beat, then said, "Derek, it's Alex. Call me—we just learned something important. Call!"

Rachel reached out and took the phone. "Let me call Greg. He should be here." She dialed his number. "Greg, it's Rachel. Look, you better come now. We just saw something incredible. Okay. Okay. On the corner of Spring and Sullivan. We'll wait."

She handed the phone back to Alex.

"What did he say?"

"He's coming. He sounded worried. I told him we'll wait right here." She saw Alex turn away, looking up and down the block. "You okay?"

Alex nodded. "Yes. I'm just scared." She laughed. "In fact I'm more scared than I've ever been."

The easiest way into the wreck was through the roof of the smashed bridge. The roof was bent down with some nasty jagged pieces, but it offered what looked like clean access to the inside of the ship.

"I see an entry point," Nick said.

Parker's voice echoed weirdly over the headset.

"Okay. That was fast. Remember the clock is running for you and me. It's like shit up here. How's your buddy doing?"

Nick turned. Philip floated nearby, his vest at a good neutral buoyancy that should let him navigate the ship. Philip paddled with hands awkwardly to the side trying to keep himself aligned . . . a lot of effort, and it had to be using up his air at an accelerated rate.

Nick picked up his own air gauge which showed still over 3000psi, then pointed at Philip.

Philip grabbed at his gauge, looked at it, and held it up to Nick.

Not how you're supposed to do it . . . but Nick swam closer.

Just fewer than 2500psi. Philip was breathing hard. They'd have to move fast. Nick pointed out the opening on the bridge. Philip nodded. Then he saw Philip dig at something on his belt. Nick hadn't noticed the chain wrapped around the priest's weight belt. Now he saw Philip pull out the small container with the host, then put it back.

In answer, Nick checked his knife.

Give me that old-time religion, he thought.

Just as they were about to enter the ship, the giant grouper floated by. Philip kicked away from the big fish, but Nick signaled him to take it easy. Groupers were big, harmless, and pretty tasty, too. The giant fish watched them with dull eyes.

Nick reached up to the headlamp on top of his mask. The light made the grouper blink—but it didn't back away.

Philip turned on his light.

One last "okay" from Nick, and then he turned around and led the way in.

As Parker battled the surf, he talked to himself. Out here, on the sea, talking to himself didn't seem weird to him at all.

"Stupid people, diving today. Near a goddamned hurricane and—"

The boat lurched left, caught in the cross-wake of two opposing swells.

Parker had to struggle to hold the wheel. He saw the rear end of the ship rise out of the water and he heard the useless groan of the propellers chopping at the air. The ship became a cork.

He looked at the radio. He wanted to tell the two divers to get the hell back up. This was worse than stupid. It was deadly.

"Won't do you any good if you surface and there's no bloody boat here!"

He heard the sound of the cell phone ringing. Who the hell is that?

"Sorry, I don't have a fucking free hand to answer the phone. Sorry." He looked at the GPS. He was far away from the drop spot, and it grew more impossible every minute to stay close.

I should tell them to surface.

Instead, he waited until the propellers hit water again and tried to play with the throttle and the wheel to stay near the divers,

Derek listened to the ringing. A weird burring noise.

"What's the matter?" Farrand said.

"The phone, it's ringing, But no answer."

"You have to do something."

Derek pressed the call button again and heard twin beeps, meaning he had a message. He pressed in his voice-mail code and heard Alex—twice.

"Is it something important?"

"My people in New York. They saw someone at this gallery, someone who wasn't supposed to be there."

"Tell them to be very careful."

Derek answered by punching in Alex's cell number. He didn't want them to do anything.

Inside the *Maroc*, the tungsten lamps all of a sudden didn't seem so powerful. The water inside the ship was filled with a million floating pieces of detritus that absorbed the brilliant light.

He turned around and checked for Philip.

The priest was using his arms to navigate the hallway. That was okay . . . just as long as he was careful not to bang his tanks riding on his back.

Nick turned forward.

A fat jellyfish glided into his mask.

Nick waved at it, but the glassine creature only wrapped around his hand, immediately filling it with stingers.

"Shit!" Nick said. The sting was immediate, and now his right hand began puffing up.

"Damn it. You there, Parker?"

Nick waited for an answer and just then he felt Philip

210

bump into him. The pain wasn't totally disabling. But it stung like hell.

"Parker, this thing on?" He waited a beat. "Shit, a lot of good the fancy communications gear did."

Just have to keep going, he knew. Down. To where they stored such ancient books of incredible power . . .

Hope it's in a crate marked "Ancient Books."

He turned back and waved at Philip, then pointed down.

Next stop—who knows?

Greg startled Rachel by coming behind her.

"You okay?" he said.

"Have you seen anything happen over there?"

"No. More people have gone in. But that's it."

"That girl must be part of it," Alex said.

"I'm sure," Greg said. "No question about it. But why?"

"We don't know," Rachel said. "But Alex called Derek in San Francisco and told him . . . warned him."

For a second a cloud seemed to cross Greg's face. As if he didn't think that was such a good thing.

"I don't think there's a lot he can do from there—"

Just then three more people climbed the steps to the gallery, looked around, and entered the door.

"What the hell are they doing over there?" Greg said. "It's weird."

He turned to Rachel and touched her. "I'm going in."

"What? You can't—"

"Look, they know you, but they don't know me."

"They don't know me either," Alex said.

Greg nodded. "Yes, but it's *my* sister that's vanished."

"But what are you going to do?"

"You still have that card?" Rachel nodded. "Then give it to me. I bet it still works."

"And leave us out here?" Alex said.

"Give me five minutes. Five minutes—and then you can

call the cops or whatever. I'll toss the card to the side after I use it. You can pick it up."

"If it works," Alex said.

"Yeah, if—but standing here is doing us no good."

Rachel thought about Nick and Philip, diving now, maybe right into a trap. If they could do something here to help, they should.

"Okay, here you go." She handed Philip the key card.

"Thanks, and wish me luck."

Rachel smiled.

Then Greg turned and walked across the street. She and Alex watched him slide the card in, wait—and then open the door. He looked at them and then tossed the card to the side as he entered the gallery.

Alex spoke up. "I'll get the card." Alex walked across the street as though she was late for a business meeting. She passed the entrance to the gallery and then stooped down matter-of-factly to pick up the key card.

She crossed the street again and doubled back to Rachel.

"Are you watching the time?" Alex said.

"Yes. Five minutes." She took a breath. "And then what?"

"We'll see . . ."

"Why won't they answer?" Farrand asked.

"Probably because they're already one hundred feet underwater."

Derek held the phone tight. This was his fifth attempt to contact the dive boat. It looked as though he was too late.

Someone answered.

At least it sounded like someone answering. Derek heard noise that he assumed was wind—but it could have been anything.

"Hello, hello? This is Derek Rayne in San Francisco."

"Hel- . . . an't . . . ear you! Keeps cutting . . ."

Damn it, this phone should be perfect anywhere on the goddamned planet.

"Is this the dive ship? Are the divers down yet?"

"-s. They are . . . own. Bad . . . here. Waves. Can't—"

What the hell was going on? It sounded as though he had called into a hurricane.

"Listen. You must tell them—"

"Again. I . . . ant hear!"

The line went dead.

He saw Farrand looking at him.

Derek's voice was quiet. He couldn't keep the sound of defeat out of his voice.

"I got to the ship, but I couldn't get the message through. Some kind of storm. Big storm."

Farrand shook his head. "The first of many, my friend. The first of many, I'm afraid."

Down one level.

Below decks.

Damn this is a tight ship, Nick thought. The passageway down the middle of the ship was so tiny. He'd have to make sure that Philip really watched his hoses dangling behind him.

He turned around to signal Philip and caught the glare of his headlamp full force, right in his eyes, blinding him.

He brought his stung hand around to shield his eyes from the brilliant glow. With his other hand, he pointed to the sides and ceiling of the passageway, and then grabbed his octopus, his spare breathing hose with a regulator.

It was so difficult to do more than vaguely suggest that he should be careful.

But Philip nodded. Maybe he understood. Maybe.

Nick grabbed his air gauge and pointed at Philip.

Philip held his own air gauge up, but in the glare it was impossible to see.

Shit, Nick thought. He'd have to curl around and kick close to gauge, in such narrow quarters.

When he felt something on his ankle.

Probably a damn eel. They love these old wrecks.

He ignored the creepy sensation for a moment.

He got closer to Philip's gauge.

1300psi. More than half his air gone. They had maybe

ten minutes to get to the crate, get the books, get them up. Pretty damn tight.

Then another sensation on his other ankle. Another eel.

He turned to face forward and looked down.

What he saw made him freeze.

At first the things on his ankles looked as though they might be some yellow-whitish fish clutching him.

But they weren't fish, they were hands, skeletal, all meat long vanished. The fingers of the hands held his ankles right above his fins. Then he looked up, as if instinct told him worse was still ahead. He was right.

Not just hands this time.

But skulls.

No cartoonlike skulls, these looked more like old sea creatures with dull eye sockets.

The hands held him, while the skulls somehow hung in the water and drifted closer.

The bony fingers dug harder into the flesh just above his ankle.

Nick fumbled for his knife. No matter how well you think you know where it is, he knew, when you're in trouble—and you go for it—you fumble.

He slipped the twelve-inch blade out of its rubber sheath. With only a glance down at the hands, he smashed the blade hard on the hands as if he might scrape them off like barnacles. But their grip only tightened, fused to him.

He heard the loud clanking sound the blade made. But it did nothing.

Looking up, the skulls were only a meter away.

And Nick thought: *This is like the shark . . . just like the shark attack.* Only now there were no hammerheads to protect him. His blade did nothing and these things were ready to rip him apart.

He felt something behind him. A hand, yanking him back.

He felt Philip pulling him close, almost hugging him.

He had almost forgotten about Philip.

If we go down, we go down together.

Not the greatest first dive.

Philip pulled him tight . . . tighter . . .

Rachel looked at the door of the gallery, then at her watch.

"Where the hell is he?" she said to Alex.

"Maybe he's talking to the director, playing detective."

"He said five minutes. It's been—God, nearly ten." She turned and looked at Alex. "I'm going in there."

"You can't do that."

"I am. Maybe Greg found something."

Alex grabbed her arm. "They know you, Rachel. You can't just—"

"Then call the police. Call 911. Give me the key card."

"Just wait a bit more."

"No. He saved me last night. Call the police. But I'm not waiting, I'm going in. Come on, Alex . . . give me the key."

Alex opened her cell phone and dialed 911. But she also handed Rachel the key card.

"Don't do anything stupid, Rachel."

Rachel took the card and headed into the gallery.

Philip held Nick tight while he extended the small silver ciborium in front.

If the host has any power, it might make them recoil, Philip thought. *That is if there is a god and he has any power in this sunken hell.*

He was gasping for breath through the regulator, looking at the skulls snapping in the light of the head lamps, closer now.

Philip held the host out as far as he could.

The skulls stopped. Nick turned around and looked at him.

See, Philip wished he could say. That old-time religion is good for something.

Now he bent down awkwardly and brought the host close to the claw hands locked on Nick's ankles. Like traps opening, the skeletal hands released, and drifted away.

In a moment there was only the murky water of this sunken tomb.

Nick looked back again and patted Philip on the shoulder, the gesture slowed by the water to a gentle, slow-motion tap. He took a look at Philip's air gauge, then brought it up to Philip's face.

900psi.

At 500 they absolutely had to turn back. That's what Nick had said.

Got to slow down my breathing, he knew. Except—even as he thought that—he knew he was breathing deep and hard, releasing great bubbles of exhaled air that dribbled to the ceiling of the passageway.

Nick pointed forward to a staircase down.

The hold.

Where would they find the books?

They were close. It was nearly over. *Please,* he thought. *Let this be over soon.*

Nick kicked away and Philip followed.

Rachel used the key and entered the gallery.

Where was everybody? All the people entered, Greg—and there was nobody here.

She retraced her steps from the night before, finding the door leading to the upper levels. She opened the door and saw the director's office, empty.

Then she heard voices, talking, animatedly. An argument? Someone fighting? She thought she heard Greg.

Was he asking about his sister? Did he forget he said five minutes?

She started up the stairs, the voices grew louder . . . sounding like people angry, accusing each other of things . . . but still Rachel couldn't make out what they were talking about.

More steps, nearly to the top, to the metal door that was muffling the noise.

Maybe Greg found something, maybe that's why he stayed. And soon the cops would be here . . .

She opened the door.

But as soon as she did the voices stopped.

As though the voices hadn't come from up here at all.

They stopped. Where was Greg . . . had something happened to him?

She told herself: *The police are coming. It's okay. I should find him, tell him.*

But where were the voices?

More steps. She said his name. "Greg?"

And he answered.

The ship's hold seemed to absorb all the light, swallowing the great powerful headlamp beams as though they were the pale yellow gasps of a dying flashlight.

Nick looked at the floating debris, the chunks of wood, the toppled crates, the cutlery, the plates, pieces of metal.

As Nick scanned the room with his light, a thought occurred to him: *Where are the fish that love to haunt dark wrecks, the eels that curl up in corners, the tiny silver fish that school in undersea tombs like this as if waiting for the sunken ship to sail?*

Where was all the life?

He saw Philip scanning the room, too.

Lots of crates here. And not much time. He could use his knife to start opening them. But he was hoping to find some marking of some kind.

ANCIENT BOOKS OF POWER IN **HERE**. RIGHT THIS WAY. If not that . . . something, some marking . . . indicating Cairo . . . something.

He kicked over to a nearby stack of crates and sent a flurry of detritus that made a filmy cloud behind him.

The stack was three crates high; the wood at the side seemed to be peeling, almost flaking like skin.

He took out his knife and poked at the topmost crate. The lid offered little resistance as Nick pried it up.

"Parker, you still up there buddy? We're in the hold. Nice cheery place filled with boxes. One of which may hold what we're looking for."

Nick didn't hear anything back.

Had the radio died? Had Parker gone back to shore disgusted with the weather.

"Parker?"

"Got you, Nick. Trying to keep my damned boat from sinking if you don't mind."

"Okay, I won't bother you with any more dive reports."

He pressed the knife into another corner of the top crate and again used the blade as a lever to make it pop up.

The top of the crate suddenly flew up.

The bloated wood was more like cardboard.

Nick sailed to the top and saw objects wrapped in gauze or muslin of some kind. Could they be the books, or some artifacts?

He felt something beside him. Philip, now beside him. Looking into the crate too . . .

Nick glanced down at Philip's gauge. 700psi.

No fucking time at all.

He sheathed his knife and reached down to the first wrapped object with his good hand. The other hand didn't sting so badly anymore but it was puffy, balloonlike.

He touched the muslin. Unlike the wood, the cloth had retained its strength.

Nick went to pick it up . . .

Derek heard the phone ring, once, twice, and then an unfamiliar voice.

"Yes?"

The voice sounded stressed and overwhelmed. Derek tried to imagine the sea the man was fighting.

"Hello . . . Listen to me. Can you talk to the divers?"

"I don't know. There's so much wind. My boat is all over the place."

"Listen to me. It's a matter of life and death. Their lives, yours. They must not bring anything up. You understand. They should—"

"What was that? Lost you at 'they must—' "

"They can't bring anything up."

Derek looked at Farrand, watching him so carefully. They were so helpless here.

"Do you understand?"

"Yes. I'll tell them . . . now."

"Thank you," Derek said.

He clicked the phone off.

"Thank you," he whispered again.

"Hm?" Farrand said. "Who was that for?"

"I'm not sure . . . God, maybe, for letting me be in time."

"And now," Farrand said, "all we have to do is wait . . ."

Nick held the wrapped object and as soon as he began unwrapping it he knew instinctively that what he held was important.

An ivory chest with Egyptian seals and mythological creatures surrounding it.

"I think I found them," Nick said.

He turned to Philip and gave a thumbs up.

"Parker we have them and we're . . ."

"Nick. Listen . . ." Parker's voice was in his ear, loud, insistent.

"Yes." Nick cradled the important object in his hands. "What is it?"

"Your boss called . . . Derek called. He said . . . 'tell them to bring nothing up.' Nothing. He said it's a matter of life and death. Shit, the boat—"

"Wait a second. Derek said that?" Nick heard nothing. "Parker?" The radio seemed dead. "Parker!" Nick yelled.

Philip watched him carefully.

He tried yelling for the divemaster one more time, but still there was no answer.

But Nick had heard the message.

And somehow it suddenly made sense.

The message was right and all this . . . was wrong.

He let the artifact tumble back into the crate.

Philip tapped him, concerned, agitated.

Nick pointed up, as in *let's go*. Now.

Philip tried to reach past him into the crate but Nick pushed him away. He tapped the headset in his facemask, and then pointed up.

Philip was still confused but Nick gave him a big push and finally his partner started to head up.

But the way up was now blocked.

• • •

Rachel stopped and turned to the sound of Greg's voice, so quiet, almost hushed as if they were in church.

"Rachel?"

She turned and saw Greg standing beside Dr. Whitney. For a moment that's all she saw, feeling so cold in this giant storeroom.

"You waited more than five minutes."

She nodded, trying to keep her thoughts straight, to see what was happening here.

"Nice of you to come up, though," Dr. Whitney said. "But where is your friend? You're not going to make us go down and get her, are you?"

Rachel looked at Greg, next to Dr. Whitney—and without special intuition, she understood that they knew each other.

"You're with them . . ." she said.

His answer was a smile. All the answer she needed. And then she permitted herself to look to the people, the creatures beside them.

They were human. Yes, she saw heads, sparkling eyes, thoughtful expressions. But she also saw everything else, the way some of them dragged something behind, a long slithery stump that could only be a tail, or how others had shoulders that curved down to claws. And how even others in the back stood erect, human-sized with the skull of some giant bird catching the dim light.

It was a freak show.

Dr. Whitney took a step closer.

"You were so . . . compliant. Followed every step, picked up every bread crumb on the trail that we laid out. It couldn't have gone better."

Rachel could barely speak. She heard the creatures shuffling, impatient. What were they waiting for, what were they promised?

"Bread crumbs . . ."

Greg nodded. "The visions got the Legacy all on the same page. That was almost too easy. But then feeding you the location of the ship, the information about the lost

220

books . . . you took all the steps with such confidence as if you were investigating—and not merely serving us."

One of the creatures to Greg's left stirred, a claw foot scraping the ground.

Impatient.

"But why us, why did you need the Legacy?"

Greg took a step closer as if what he was about to say was some kind of secret.

"The ship had a ward on it, a sacred ward. It was protected for all time. Certainly there was no way we could survive a journey into the hold."

Rachel's mind was racing . . . trying to understand all this.

Maroc was protected. The books were safe. Unless—

Philip. He could bring the power of the Church, to penetrate that ship.

She felt sick, dizzy, as though she could collapse on the floor.

She thought of those claw feet.

She looked at Greg. "But what about your sister?"

"My sister? My lost sister?"

He turned around. Behind him stood the giant sarcophagus. Greg walked back to it. He grabbed the lid and tugged on it, hard. The lid creaked open slowly.

And Rachel saw Martina. She was encased in some kind of form-fitting glass covering, as though she had been dipped in glass and trapped in a glass bodysuit.

She was right here, all the time.

What were her words . . .

Rachel said them aloud.

"I am not lost . . ."

"Hm," Greg said. "Oh, yes—what Martina said. That was one problem we had. We could trap her in this zone between life and death, and use her to draw the Legacy closer. But one thing we didn't know was that she could give you a message we weren't prepared for. Still, it did no good."

"Your own sister . . ."

At those words Greg took a step forward and brought a

fist up to Rachel's face. He began muttering words in a language whose every strangeness spoke of worlds and millennia away.

The last word he virtually spit at Rachel's face.

"Horus!"

The creatures by his side began to move. Greg's smile broadened. What was about to happen was clearly something he was looking forward to.

Rachel backed up into one of the tall shelves, with nowhere to go.

Nick looked at Philip. In front of them, alien creatures blocked their way. Things far worse than any shark. After all, what shark had tendril-like hands protruding from its body?

Another creature—a giant eel—had, at one end, what looked like a tiny human head ringed with teeth.

Nick felt himself gasping.

One of the eel things lashed out at him, snapping at his leg, ripping thorough the neoprene, filling the murky water with a bloody fog.

Then another one tried the same maneuver, but this time Nick used his knife to slice it in two. For a moment it writhed—a worm cut in two for bait. Then the rear end sprouted another head, and now two of the human-eels danced in front of him.

A lot of fucking good his knife was doing.

He saw Philip wrestling with one of the eel things while the shark-with-hands came closer.

God, how much air can Philip have?

He had to be down to 200psi. If that.

"Parker, we're in deep shit down here. Parker, can you hear me?"

No answer on the radio.

No answer, because they were alone, 120 feet down in a sunken madhouse. More blooms of blood sprouted, this time from Philip wrestling with an eel.

The shark thing lunged, but not at Philip. Instead, Nick watched it cleverly feint running straight, then curve around. The little dwarf hands reached out for him.

But this time Nick took his knife and jabbed the blade dead on the snout of the shark thing.

And supernatural or not, the creature from hell reared back.

Pain is pain. Everywhere.

It's a fucking universal.

He looked over. Philip was covered with the eel things. And worse. Far worse. No air bubbles.

He was out of air.

Poor padre. Pray to your god. Because that's all we have left.

Through the bloody fog, Nick could see the shark thing coming closer, the long knife sticking up from its snout.

I'm out of weapons. Out of hope. If I believed in God, I'd pray too. Maybe it's not too late.

He heard something. A banging, a clanking. Loud, then louder. Finally a great crash.

The murky, reddish water blew away as some fresh current shot into the room.

Nick turned around.

He saw a diver. It took a second for him, totally stunned, to see Parker.

He had an ax in his hand. Amazing how handy an ax could be.

He planted the ax in the shark thing.

Nick pointed to Philip, wrestling with the eel things.

But Parker was already there, dragging Nick out of the hole he had made in the weakened hull with the ax. And Nick watched, as soon as Philip crossed the exterior of the hull, how the eels peeled away. They could't come out.

Nick kicked right after them.

He felt an eel quickly curl around his ankle then uncurl as Nick sailed through the opening.

They were out to where the water was clear.

Parker had Philip on his octopus, breathing air. He didn't waste any time heading to the surface.

Nick followed, maybe pushing the limit of a foot per second, maybe going a bit too fast.

He'd worry about nitrogen buildup later.

And then—as if it was a dream—they were on the surface, still stormy, still dotted with whitecaps.

Nick hit his BC, filling it with air, then spit out his regulator. He watched Parker inflate Philip's vest. The priest looked dazed, as though he had gone a good minute with nothing to breathe.

"Where's your boat?"

Parker looked around. The he pointed left, and shouted. "I locked the steering wheel in a circular turn. Just have to swim close to a moving bouncing boat and catch the railing! Piece of cake."

Parker had to gauge when to kick close, grab the railing, and hold on while he climbed aboard. It didn't help that the boat bounced up and down, belly flopping every few seconds.

Nick swam close to Philip.

"You okay, Padre?"

Philip nodded. "I've got bites . . . all over."

"Me, too. But we're alive."

Philip smiled then. "I guess prayer does work, eh?"

And Nick laughed.

Derek waited with Farrand quietly, the two of them trapped by their inability to do anything, to imagine what was happening.

Derek started to say something, "Tell me, do you—"

His phone rang. He flipped it open. And heard Nick's voice, Nick alive. On the surface.

Incredible.

Greg spoke. "The books have been liberated. Now all we have to do is kill you. Give our little group some fun here . . ."

But the door opened behind Rachel and she turned to see Alex, her phone in her hand.

"The police are coming," Alex said.

Dr. Whitney laughed. "Do you know what the response

time is in New York? You will both be gone by the time any police come here."

But Alex took a step right up to the group of monstrosities.

"The books are still there."

Rachel turned from Alex to Greg. His face looked horrified.

Alex went on. "The books are there, still sunken. Your plan failed. They remain . . . protected."

There was a stirring in the group. And when Rachel looked at Alex, she sensed something. Alex had become aware of something she could use against them.

"And these monsters . . . your followers. They have traded their humanity . . . not to be gods . . . but to be trapped forever, as they are."

More stirring. A snort. Claws scraping the wooden floor.

Dr. Whitney looked around.

"They traded their immortal souls to become twisted monsters and now there's no way out for them, no way to the 'next level' you promised them."

Rachel kept watching Alex, her voice strong, powerful. Maybe she was even sending an image, a thought, some idea to the creatures.

Or maybe they didn't need it.

They had been betrayed.

Trapped.

The thing with the bird head took a step from the background. *God, he's going to attack us,* Rachel thought.

But when the bird-human was under the light, it reached out and planted its curved beak in Greg's shoulder blade.

And Greg's scream acted like a signal.

They all swarmed around the two leaders, and began biting and clawing and chewing, covering the floor with blood.

Alex grabbed Rachel's hand. "Quick. They'll probably turn on each other next, but we can't bet on that."

Rachel shook her head. "Hold on!"

She grabbed a giant stone statue, some Egyptian deity carved out of blue faïence. She ran to the sarcophagus, opened it, and then smashed the stone against the glass covering Martina.

The thin glass covering Martina shattered into a thousand tiny shards.

Some of those shards flew back at Rachel and Alex, others stuck to Martina.

Was she dead? Was she still suspended in this dream-world?

But then she opened her eyes, such beautiful eyes.

Behind them, the carnage continued as creature ripped at creature.

"Quick, come with us," Rachel said.

She took the dazed girl's hand, and pulled her out of the coffin, to the metal door, running as fast as they could.

EPILOGUE

They all met in the conference room of Legacy Center, sitting around the table as if this was a meeting of the board of some powerful conglomerate.

But Derek knew this . . .

What had happened was a great lesson to the Legacy.

The Legacy could be tricked and used. Illusion and reality could be twisted.

The other side, the forces of darkness, could be incredibly clever.

This time, they had orchestrated events so the Legacy could get something for them that they couldn't get themselves.

Philip's holy orders, his sacred host, was able to penetrate the ward.

And what if the books had been brought to the surface?

The war would be truly joined. The gateway to the alternate universe ruled by the twisted depravities some called gods, would be open.

It chilled Derek to think about it.

He looked around the table. Philip was talking to Farrand, Nick to Alex. They were like shell-shocked troops. Only now they knew exactly how mortal they were.

"I don't . . ." Derek started, speaking quietly, ". . . want to keep anyone here very long. Father Farrand—" He called the man priest even though Farrand thought he had left that behind. Some forms of priesthood you just can't give up. "—I want to thank you again for what you did. For us. For the world."

"Thank yourselves," Farrand said. "And I can tell you one thing. I will sleep better at night knowing that you exist. Though—" he laughed "—sleep won't come too easy."

Derek turned to Nick and Phil, sitting close together. Had they made their peace with each other? Would Philip rejoin the Legacy? It was a question for another day.

"Nick, Philip . . . how are your wounds?"

"Healing," Philip said. "I won't be jogging for some months."

"Me, too. These wounds will probably leave the weirdest looking scars I've ever seen."

Derek nodded.

"Alex, has there been anything on the LDN, any fallout from this incident?"

"Only this—the police did show up. They found the blood, the dead creatures. I think they put some kind of cover story about a cult sacrifice, implicating the gallery director. And Martina is doing well at home. She remembers nothing about how she was put into the dream state, trapped in that netherworld. I told her to watch her dreams and stay in touch. Apparently she's planning a trip to Russia with her parents."

"And her brother? What do they know—"

Rachel answered. "I went to them. I told them . . . how he helped free her. How he was killed. I figured it was best."

"Yes. Absolutely. And how are you, Rachel? You got more than you bargained for in your trip to New York?"

"Yes. No more conferences for me. Unless they're in Hawaii."

"Hey," Nick said. "I'm with you. The diving there is incredible . . ."

"I think I'm done with diving," Philip said. "Way too dangerous."

More laughter.

This was good, Derek thought. Laughing about the horror. They seem to go together. The fear . . . then this release. Laughing at death.

But as he sat there he knew the day would come when one of them would be lost in the battle.

He knew that would happen.

A secret that he carried with him.

Farrand spoke. "I guess I should get ready. Flying back in a few hours."

"To England?" Derek asked.

"No. Italy. The Vatican. Some people there I want to thank. Who knows—they may be able to recruit me again."

"Thank you," Derek said. "For everything. And I hope you will become part of our net of allies."

"I'd be insulted if you didn't ask." He looked around the room at the computer terminals. "But tell me—do I have to learn how to use a computer? I'm too old for that!"

He looked around the table, with a face that recognized the absurdity of what he just said . . . in light of what he had just done.

He started laughing, and soon everyone was.